MANU

HELL SQUAD #16

ANNA HACKETT

Manu

Published by Anna Hackett

Copyright 2018 by Anna Hackett

Cover by Melody Simmons of eBookindiecovers

Edits by Tanya Saari

ISBN (ebook): 978-1-925539-47-9

ISBN (paperback): 978-1-925539-48-6

Hell Squad – Amazon Bestselling Science Fiction Romance Series and SFR Galaxy Award for best Post-Apocalypse for Readers who don't like Post-Apocalypse

The Anomaly Series – #1 Amazon Action Adventure Romance Bestseller

Sign up for my VIP mailing list and get your *free box set* containing three action-packed romances.

Visit here to get started:
www.annahackettbooks.com

CHAPTER ONE

S he loved the feel of a carbine in her hands.

Kate Scott paused, her gaze scanning the rolling, green field ahead. It wasn't that she liked killing people. As a career Army officer, and now head of the security team at the Enclave, it was more that she liked knowing she could handle whatever came her way.

Especially if it was an alien raptor.

Her hands tightened on her weapon. Nope, she didn't mind killing the Gizzida. The aliens had invaded Earth two years ago and promptly decimated the planet. All the cities were in ruins, and most of the planet's population was dead. Any survivors were fighting for their lives, or held in captivity, enslaved by the raptors.

Kate pulled in a deep breath, then released it slowly. This pretty, green field was south of Sydney—once the bright, busy capital of the United Coalition—and didn't give any clue to the devastation the rest of the planet had suffered.

Beneath her, far underground, lay the Enclave—a purpose-built sanctuary for human survivors. Built by the lying, murdering, and thankfully, now-dead former president. For over a year, Kate had lived here, thinking she'd been on the righteous side of the fight.

Until survivors from Blue Mountain Base had arrived. Men and women who'd been busy fighting back and saving others, while Kate had been blissfully hiding out. Old guilt nipped at her. It didn't matter that the survivors were now fully integrated into the Enclave, and that they were all working together to fight the aliens and survive. She hated that she'd been an ignorant fool.

"It's so nice to be out in the sunshine."

The voice beside her made Kate turn her head. Kendra was a new member of Kate's team. The young blonde had begged and pestered Kate until Kate had allowed her to join. Right now, decked out in carbon fiber that made her look like she was playing dress-up, the young woman had her head tipped up to the blue sky.

Kendra smiled. "I love the safety of the Enclave, but I miss the sun and fresh air sometimes."

"Enjoy it, but stay focused," Kate said.

The young woman's smile faded and she nodded. "Of course."

Kate stifled a sigh. Pre-invasion, Kendra would still be at university, going to parties, dating, and pondering her career choices. There was a bright, eager look on the young woman's fresh face. God, she made Kate feel ancient. Kate had joined the Army straight out of school, gotten her engineering degree, then lowered her head and made a career in service to the Coalition.

She'd been good at it. The order, structure, and sense of purpose had suited her.

After her disastrous and short-lived engagement at twenty-eight, the years had somehow whizzed by. Before she'd known it, she'd been in her late thirties. She'd turned down several promotions to stay in the job she'd loved. And while she'd dated off and on, she'd never felt fireworks. She'd never met a man she'd wanted to keep around or start a family with.

Her fingers tensed on the metal of her carbine. Looking back, the men she'd dated had been good men, well-matched, but they'd never been... hot-blooded or wild with desire for her. Kate had long ago accepted that she was not a passionate woman.

When she'd been selected for a special operation providing presidential protection, at first she'd been honored and thrilled. It had come at just the right time. Her gut curdled. She'd had a mission under her command go wrong—horribly wrong. She'd been ready for a change. As it turned out, President Howell had fooled them all. She'd protected and defended the bastard, and all the while, he'd been bargaining with the aliens to ensure his own comfort and survival. And he'd tossed the rest of humanity under the bus in the process.

"Captain?"

Kate blinked at Kendra. Shit, she'd just warned the woman to stay focused and here Kate was, ruminating.

"Let's keep moving," Kate said. "We need to check the security around all the Enclave entrances."

Kendra's shoulders straightened. "Yes, Captain."

They skirted a clump of trees, checking the Enclave's

hidden entrances. Kate studied the ground, ensuring there was no sign of the Gizzida or any tampering.

The aliens knew the general location of the base, and unfortunately, they'd even made it inside once. After that incident, Kate had worked hard to block that part of the Enclave off, and ensure the rest of the main base was safe.

She walked onward, the grass crunching under her boots. She frowned. In most places, the grass was long and lush, but in this patch, the grass was dried and brown. She looked up and spotted another patch not far away. Had to be bugs, or something, probably.

Scanning their surroundings once more, she looked beyond another stand of trees, branches swaying gently in the breeze. This area, not far from the coastal city of Wollongong, had been a former coal mining area. The Enclave itself had been built in an old mine. In the distance, she could see the rusted ruins of an old processing plant from a neighboring mine.

"Captain, I wanted to thank you again," Kendra said.

Kate looked up. "For what?"

"For letting me join the security team. I've been wanting to do something to help for so long, and I know I'm young and inexperienced—"

"You'll learn," Kate said. "And you shouldn't thank me. It can be a tough job."

Kendra nodded. "I know. But I'm helping keep the Enclave safe and protect my family." Kendra was one of the lucky ones who had her parents and sisters alive and with her. "So, thank you."

God, the young woman was thanking her for letting

her work hard and risk her life. The world was such a mess.

Something rustled in the trees.

Kate whipped her carbine up and saw Kendra do the same. Kate's heart thumped as she stared down the sight of her weapon. Kendra's fast breathing was loud but the woman was still. Lifting a hand, Kate gave a signal, and together they moved forward.

"Shit," Kendra muttered.

Kate looked over and saw the woman studying her carbine. "What's wrong?" Kate moved her gaze back to the trees. The rustling was louder now.

"The laser pack on my carbine just died." The woman's voice was panicked. "I've got nothing."

Kate scowled. "Did you check it before we left?"

"Of course."

"Pull out your backup pistol and stay behind me." Kate touched a hand to her earpiece. "Enclave, are the drones picking up any alien activity?"

"Nothing, Captain." The polite, feminine voice belonged to Elle Steele, one of the comms officers. "All clear."

Suddenly, a kangaroo burst out of the trees, bounding across the grass with a powerful flex of its legs. It didn't even look in their direction. Kate lowered her weapon, shaking her head.

Kendra gave a nervous laugh.

As the animal bounded away, Kate glanced down at her carbine. As she watched, the lights flickered out on her laser cartridge.

What the hell?

She lifted it and pulled the trigger. Nothing. Her heart slammed against her ribs. One carbine failing was possible. It happened. They worked hard to maintain their equipment, but they no longer had an endless supply of new gear or parts. But two weapons failing at the same time...

Kate didn't believe in coincidences. She examined her carbine and confirmed that it was dead.

"Enclave, our weapons are malfunctioning. We're heading back to the western entrance."

"Acknowledged," Elle said. "The relief patrol will meet you there."

"Thanks, Elle." Kate glanced over at Kendra, anger churning in her gut. She hated the idea of them being stuck out here with no protection. Damn sitting ducks. "I'll take these weapons to get checked out."

Kate stomped through the grass. Out here, malfunctioning weapons could mean death. And to top it all off, she now needed to head down to the armory attached to the Enclave firing range and see the man who ran it.

Her body tightened, her muscles vibrating with tension. She had no idea why, but just the thought of this one particular man affected her in ways she didn't want, and certainly didn't like.

Get the job done, Kate. Drop the weapons off. Easy.

She gave herself a mental shake. She always did her job, no matter what. She'd concentrate on the malfunctioning weapons and not the big, muscled man who elicited unwelcome, annoying, and frankly uncomfortable feelings inside her.

Suddenly, she sensed something. "Down." She

waved at Kendra and they both dropped to the grassy ground.

Kate scanned the sky and saw a plume of dark smoke in the air, rushing in their direction. Her pulse spiked, then she saw a shimmer and realized what it was.

A Hawk was incoming with its illusion system up, but it had been hit. She watched it pass overhead and she scanned again, making sure there wasn't an alien ship on its tail.

Not that she could do much with a useless weapon in her hand.

No alien ptero ships appeared. The sky was clear and blue.

She lifted her chin. "Let's go." She had a weapons expert to chew out.

THE HAWK QUADCOPTER barreled through the narrow ravine. The rock walls looked so close he felt like he could reach out and touch them.

Damn, Erickson was a hell of a pilot. Manu Rahia tightened his grip on the autoturret he was sitting in and drew in a deep breath.

"Aliens still on our fucking tail?" Hemi, Manu's brother, called out.

Manu focused. The airspace behind them was clear. "Nope. Think my last shot took that ptero down."

A hand slapped Manu's back. "You are a hell of a shot, bro." Hemi's grin was wide and white in his bronze face. He was built like a tank, his dark hair pulled back in a stubby ponytail. "Just like old times."

A feeling like sludge moved through Manu's gut. "Yeah."

Except it wasn't. He wasn't a berserker anymore. Damn, it hurt to admit just how much he'd missed this. Missed being out there fighting the aliens face to face.

He turned his head, taking in his brothers and the rest of his old squad in the quadcopter. His younger brother, Tane, the squad's leader, stood still, gaze zeroed out the side window. Alert and prepared, that described Tane perfectly. He was tall and lean, his dreadlocks pulled back from his face.

Hemi was leaning against the wall beside Manu, grinning. Hemi laughed a lot, even more since he'd tumbled head-over-ass in love with Camryn McNab from Squad Nine. The passionate pair certainly kept things interesting. For all his humor, Manu knew his brother was far more perceptive than he let on.

Manu smiled. He was damn lucky to have his brothers here. So many had lost all their loved ones in the invasion. Family was the most important thing to him. An acute pain cut at him. Pain for his big, sprawling family back in New Zealand. He dragged in a breath. His ma and step-father had raised three wild boys to be men who gave a shit and loved their family. Manu had tried contacting the area where his parents had lived and gotten nothing. And then there'd also been his extended family—aunts, uncles, cousins.

His hands curled into fists. He knew they couldn't all

have made it, and the thought fucking killed him. *Bastard aliens.*

He looked back at his brothers. He had to look after the family he had right here. He'd always known that the good-natured Hemi would gladly take a tumble for the right woman. He'd made a hell of a good choice in the long, sexy Cam. His gaze switched to Tane.

His youngest brother was a different story. Hard and composed, Tane had done shit as a mercenary, shit he'd never talked about, and it had changed him. Once, as a good-looking teenager, he'd smiled a lot, but he'd come back from the jungles of South America a different man. Working as a mercenary had knocked the soft edges out of Tane, and left something sharp and honed in their place.

Manu liked to think that, in time, Tane would still find a woman who'd soften him again and give him some beauty, some comfort, and most of all, love. But the alien invasion had made the odds of that a lot stiffer.

But, there were lots of people who were beating the odds. On the seats at the back of the Hawk, the rest of the berserkers sat. Former cop and ex-con Griff Callan had his eyes closed and beside him, former Mafia enforcer Dom Santora sat even stiller than Tane. The dark-haired man always reminded Manu of a snake coiled and ready to strike. He trusted both men with his life. In the row behind them, Levi King and Ash Connors sat, both of the former bikers laughing about something. Considering both men had just claimed two of the prettiest women in the Enclave as theirs, it wasn't surprising they looked relaxed and happy, even though they'd just been under fire.

Squad Three, known as the berserkers, were rough and tough. They played hard and fought harder...fighting back against the Gizzida aliens who'd invaded, destroyed, and were still fighting to control the Earth.

Manu had been a berserker too. He looked down. In his carbon fiber armor, it was impossible to tell one of his legs was made of metal and alloy. Impossible to tell that the fucking aliens had destroyed a piece of him.

"We're clear," Finn Erickson called from the cockpit. "Nice shooting back there. We only got hit once."

Manu craned his neck and spotted the plume of smoke behind them. "Critical?"

"Nah," Finn replied. "I'll just have to put up with the bitching from the Hawk maintenance team."

"And some teasing from your woman," Levi added. "Over who's the better pilot."

Finn laughed. "That, too."

Finn's woman, Lia, was head of the drone team. Manu thought the guy didn't sound too cut up about her teasing him.

"When you asked me on this mission, you didn't say we'd get shot at and chased by pteros," a deep voice said.

Manu looked at the final occupant of the Hawk. Noah Kim ran the tech team back at the Enclave.

"Suck it up, Kim," Hemi said. "It's good for you to get out of your geek lab occasionally."

Noah snorted and crossed his arms over his chest. "I like my lab."

"I appreciate you guys coming." Tane looked at Noah, then at Manu.

Manu shrugged. "We didn't help much."

This had been a recon mission. A few weeks back, the berserkers had discovered a strange alien device—a black octagon—hidden in a submerged dome off Botany Bay. No one knew what the hell it was, just that the Gizzida were trying to keep it a secret, and in all likelihood, it was a weapon. A weapon to wipe out the last surviving pockets of humanity.

Problem was, since that mission, the aliens had moved the fucking octagon and no one knew where it was.

"That black glass certainly looked Gizzida to me," Manu said.

They'd just investigated a site in the Blue Mountains, where the Enclave drones had picked up an area where the trees had all been flattened by...something. In the center of it, had been black glass and the twisted, burned remains of something that looked and smelled Gizzida.

Manu, who now ran the armory and firing range, had come to offer his weapons expertise. Noah, who was a genius with all things electronic, had come to help as well.

A sense of unease moved through Manu. He was pretty certain what they'd seen in the mountains had been a test site. The aliens had tested something ugly.

They had the remains of whatever the hell it was in a strong box in the back of the Hawk. Manu and Noah would get to work analyzing it when they got back.

What they hadn't expected was to find themselves

face to face with three alien ptero ships intent on taking them down.

"Those pteros didn't know what hit them," Levi called out.

Manu smiled and cracked his knuckles. Of course, all three pteros were now steaming piles of ruin. Damn, it felt so good to be back out on a Hawk. A burn of anger and resentment cut through him, heavily layered with grief.

He loved working at the firing range. He had a good team, and when he wasn't busy maintaining weapons, he was studying the aliens' toys and tinkering with his own weapon designs.

But it wasn't the same as being out here, taking down the aliens. No matter how much he might wish things were different, he wasn't a berserker anymore.

"Manu, you are the shit on that turret," Ash added.

Manu lifted his chin. Except he knew someone even better than him. His thoughts went back a few weeks. To when he'd taken a ragtag group of volunteers out to provide support to the berserkers on the deadly dome mission.

He'd stood in a Hawk beside a certain head of Enclave security and watched her work the autoturret like a virtuoso.

Captain Kate Scott, of the fit body, poised face, and huge blue eyes. She screamed sensible, tough, and dedicated to her job. Except for her lips. Manu smiled. The woman had full lips that were made for sin.

"Manu?"

He blinked and saw Tane studying him. He cleared his throat. "Yeah."

"What were you thinking about?"

"Taking down aliens."

Tane tilted his head, one of his dreadlocks falling over his broad shoulder. "No, you weren't."

Damn, sometimes it was annoying having brothers who knew him so well.

"Welcome home, gents," Finn Erickson called out from the cockpit.

Manu glanced out the window and saw a field of green grass ahead. Below it, was the Enclave—home to several hundred humans trying to survive this alien apocalypse.

Hemi dropped into a seat. "Home. That means a hot shower, a beer, and my woman."

As the others laughed, Manu looked at the checkplate floor. His gut hardened. He was happy to be home, even if he was missing the woman part of Hemi's equation, but a part of him didn't want to get off the Hawk. A part of him wanted to savor this moment.

But as he always did, he shook off the feeling. He had an important job to do at the Enclave and he was sure as hell going to do it to the best of his ability.

CHAPTER TWO

Manu strode into the firing range, still in his armor, his heavy carbine slung over his shoulder. He needed to shower and change, but he wanted to check on his team first.

He strode through an adjoining door, past his office and into the back room.

A young man was hunched over one of the benches, absorbed in his work. Two long benches filled the room. Weapons in various states of repair were laid out on the shiny surface. Some were fully assembled, some in pieces while being overhauled.

Racks lined the walls, and all of them were loaded with carbines, laser pistols, combat knives, grenades, and more. All weapons that had been scavenged, salvaged, and recovered.

"You're back, boss," Alex called out. "How'd it go?"

"Shot down some alien pteros, and brought back some alien glass, and who knows what else, to examine."

Alex nodded. "Cool."

Manu leaned over the bench, checking out the weapon Alex was cleaning. "Don't forget the cartridge slot grooves. Give 'em a little extra elbow grease."

Alex smiled. "You got it, Manu. Can't believe how much I'm learning from you."

Manu grunted. The Enclave had been well-stocked when they'd arrived here, but with the squads out there fighting every day, they were always running low on things. In the corner of the room, a 3D printer was chugging away, making some replacement parts.

He was doing his best to keep the weapons in top-notch form for the squads. No way in hell his brothers or the other soldiers would go down because of defective weapons.

"Keep working on those carbines, Alex. I'll check in with you later."

The man gave him a salute, and Manu walked through the door into the firing range. Several of the long lanes were currently occupied.

Big, broad Roth Masters, the leader of Squad Nine, was in one lane firing a carbine. Each laser discharge hit the target dead center. His woman, Avery, was in the next lane with a pistol, and Squad Nine's second, Mac, was busy firing a shotgun. The boom of the weapon reverberated through the space.

The trio finished firing, and all three pulled their targets up to check. Avery pumped a hand into the air with a grin. Manu watched Roth yank his woman in for a hard kiss while Mac shook her head and laughed.

Life went on. Even when aliens were trying to end it.

Turning away from the trio, Manu moved through the firing range, scanning the area and checking on his employees. He liked running a tight ship. As he walked, his left leg throbbed.

He'd clearly overdone it today. A painful reminder of why he wasn't a berserker anymore.

And never would be again.

He gritted his teeth, the ugly memories of that brutal mission rising. It had happened right before they'd been forced to abandon Blue Mountain Base.

As he walked, he could feel where his prosthetic met the skin of his thigh. The high-tech alloy leg was grafted onto his own. His brothers had disobeyed orders and scavenged the best prosthetic they could find, but he wouldn't again leap from a Hawk quadcopter or run into a battle.

Not unless things were completely fucked and there were no soldiers left to fight.

He forced himself to look around the range, taking in the lanes and the weapons. His new job was important, too. He knew that, even if he did still feel a tiny seed of resentment that he wasn't out there with his squad, fighting and protecting his brothers' backs.

Manu relaxed his hands. He never let that tiny seed take root. Keeping the soldiers in weapons was a damn important job, and he was going to fucking do it well.

At the end of the day, he'd lost some skin and bone. Others had lost far more, including their lives and everything that had mattered to them. He had a high-tech prosthetic, could function well, and still had a purpose. Life went on. You adapted, pivoted, and rolled with the punches.

There was a sharp bang as the door to the firing range slammed open.

He turned his head and saw a tall woman striding in, a carbine clutched in each hand.

Manu watched and let himself savor the little spike he felt in his pulse. Captain Kate Scott could certainly make his day more interesting.

He rarely saw her smile, and he'd never heard her laugh. He wondered just what it would take to have her tip that head back and laugh. Although, truth be told, that wasn't the only reaction he'd like to get from her.

"What kind of shoddy work are you doing down here, Rahia?" Her face was tight.

He raised his eyebrows. He was used to her cool expressions and composed replies. "Good afternoon to you, too, Captain."

She pulled in a breath, then shoved one of the carbines at his chest. "When I'm out on patrol, I don't need defective weapons."

"Defective?" He took the carbine, glancing down at it.

She held out the other one. "Both failed on patrol."

Manu frowned. He could see the laser cartridges were offline. "Let me take a look—"

Kate slammed her hands on her hips. "I do not need to be facing down raptors with a weapon that doesn't work."

Manu felt another spike in his blood. "Did a raptor climb up your ass while you were out there?"

Her eyes widened. "You did not just say that."

"Cool it, Kate. Let me get to the bottom of this." He lifted the carbines, ejecting the cartridges. He walked over to his desk at the back of the range, touched his comp, and pulled up the records of the weapons.

"I had a new team member with me. A young woman who's put her life in my hands."

Ah, now Manu was getting why the usually unflappable captain was riled. "These were in perfect working order when they were checked out."

She straightened, her brow creasing.

"What the hell did you do to them?" he asked.

Her gaze narrowed. "Nothing. Kendra's flickered and went out. Mine followed a few minutes later."

She was standing close to him, and at this distance, Manu could smell her. Damn, she smelled good. Like soap and carbon fiber. This close, he could see her hair was thick and shiny, brushing her strong jawline. And she had that lush mouth that was so at odds with her personality. Lips that gave a man ideas.

"I'll investigate," he told her. "And I'll have my guys pull these apart and check all the other carbines, as well."

She visibly tried to relax. "Good. I don't want this happening again."

He grabbed her arm and felt her muscles tense under his fingers. "Said I'd do it and I will."

"It should never have happened in the first place."

"Yeah, I get that, and I said I'll find out what happened. What's gotten into you?"

Her lips flattened and she tried to pull away. "Nothing. I'm just angry."

"The cool, composed Captain Scott angry? First time for everything, I guess."

She gave the slightest flinch, then rounded on him. "I want to ensure my team members stay safe. I won't have them injured in the field because you're down here sitting on your ass and not doing your job right."

Now, it was Manu's turn to stiffen. "Because with a bum leg, I'm incapable of doing anything, right?"

Her face changed, eyes widening. "That's not what I—"

Bad feelings churned in his gut. He turned away from her. "I'll update you once I know more."

"Rahia." Her voice had changed.

"I said I'd update you when I know more."

She took a step closer. "I see you're in armor, so I'm guessing you've been out with the berserkers for something."

"They dust me off and let me out sometimes," he bit out.

Her face softened. "You miss it."

God. He crossed his arms over his chest. He didn't want to dissect this with her.

She blew out a breath. "I was on that mission with you, remember? When we went in to help your brothers and their squad. I *know* what you can do."

Fuck. He'd taken out his frustration on her. He scraped a hand through his hair. "Kate—"

"Let me know about the carbines." With that, she spun and strode out.

Manu muttered another curse. *That went well.*

KATE MARCHED out of the firing range and down the corridor. As soon as she'd turned a corner, she stopped and leaned her back against the wall. She let her head thud against the concrete and closed her eyes. *God.*

Her body was on fire. She felt like fire ants were crawling over her skin. She loosened the top button of her shirt. She'd *never* felt like this before.

All because of *him.*

Behind her closed lids, she instantly pictured Manu. Big. Muscled. Strong. His skin was dark-bronze, and he had a hint of an interesting Maori-style tattoo peeking out from under his sleeve.

She'd had an okay, if uninspired, sex life before the invasion. Sure, it hadn't been frequent, but she'd never really had a strong sex drive. She'd never felt so...hot and bothered before.

Opening her eyes, she stared blindly at the wall. *Why him?* Okay, his strength was attractive. His skills were undeniable. His smile...

Ahh. She was losing her mind. Kate pushed away from the wall and set off down the corridor again. She was Kate Scott. Dependable. Steady. She didn't go off half-cocked, and especially not because of a man. She wasn't a hormone-driven twenty-something.

Except, because she was so busy trying to hide how she was feeling, she'd nearly ripped Manu's head off over the carbines. She shook her head. She had work to do.

After a meeting with Niko, the civilian leader of the Enclave, who she liked and respected, Kate found herself in the gym, watching her team train. She had quite a few new recruits and she put them through rigorous training before she let them out in the field.

She watched a man and woman race up the climbing wall, cataloging their strengths and weaknesses—strong legs, weak upper body strength, good balance, excellent strategy. They reminded her so strongly of some of the young soldiers she'd trained in the Army.

Soldiers who'd bled out in the sand in a Middle Eastern desert.

Her gut cramped, her vision blurring. For a second, she felt the sweat sliding down her back under her fatigues, blinding sun in her eyes, and the screams of her dying people in her ears.

"Kate?"

The male voice snapped her back to the Enclave gym. She stared blindly at Miles, her second-in-command. He was watching her carefully, his tank top soaked in sweat. He was a few years younger than her, with a head of blond hair and perpetual stubble on his strong jaw. He was also solid and dependable.

"Sorry. Lost in my thoughts."

"Not pleasant ones."

She didn't share. She was the boss, and she had to ensure her people knew she was steady, strong, someone they could lean on and trust. "Just want to make sure these recruits have the skills they need to do the job." And stay alive.

Miles grinned. "You know they curse your training programs behind your back."

She nodded. "Good."

Kate had never cared about being liked or being socia-ble. She'd take tough but fair. And she'd take all her people having the skills they needed to thrive at their jobs.

"Okay, everyone, to the weights," she called out. "I have a circuit set up."

There were good-natured groans and Kate hid a smile. Instead, she stared at them until everyone snapped to attention and grabbed some weights.

Again, she watched them move through the stations, making notes in her head. People who needed a little extra training. Some who were ready to head out on patrol.

She heaved out a breath. Frustration was still eating at her from her encounter with Manu. She eyed the treadmills. After she was finished with her team, she might run this edgy feeling off.

She looked back to her people. "Okay, everyone. That's it. Good work. Head out and hit the showers."

They herded past her, and she listened to their laughter and conversation. After their showers, they'd head to the dining room. Most people at the Enclave would be there, spending time with their families and friends. Blowing off steam, feeling that sense of connection.

Her jaw clenched tight. She had a date with a treadmill.

But running mindless kilometers on the treadmill until she was drenched with sweat still didn't do the trick. The unfamiliar edginess was still riding her. She took a quick shower and headed back to her office.

As soon as she entered her space, she saw the carbine resting on her desk. A note sat beside it.

She stared at the bold masculine script and her pulse spiked.

Your carbine. Minor issue with the program. Now re-aligned. M

Kate dropped into her chair and snatched the note up. She stroked a finger over the letters.

Huffing out a breath, she finally admitted to herself that she was attracted to Manu Rahia.

She'd watched him for weeks down at the firing range. Hell, the chance to see him was one of the reasons she went down there so much. Once again, her skin felt tight and hot. She leaned back in her chair. It wasn't really him, she tried to convince herself. It was just that she'd been alone a long time. It'd been so long since someone had touched her.

She blew out a breath. She couldn't let sexual frustration be a problem. She just needed to find a way to shake this tension, and then Manu would simply be a work colleague, like all the others. She needed to solve this issue like every other challenge she'd come up against.

There was a knock at her door and she looked up.

A freshly showered Miles stood in her doorway. He lifted a brow. "Coming for a beer?"

She managed a smile, although it felt like a grimace. "I have some work—"

"No, Kate." The man shook his head. "You almost always avoid team drinks. In case you missed it, we're in the middle of an alien invasion. A cohesive team is important, and you don't have to be 'stoic Kate' all the time."

The name hit a little too close to her nickname in the Army. Stone Heart Scott. No one said it to her face, but she'd heard the whispers. She'd always shrugged it off before, but now, it felt like salt in a wound she didn't know she had.

"Doesn't Lauren want you home?"

"My girlfriend understands that I need to hang with my team." A wide smile. "She'll be waiting for me."

Must be nice to know someone was waiting. *Blow off some steam, Kate. Relax.* "Okay," she agreed reluctantly. "I have time for one drink."

CHAPTER THREE

K ate followed Miles into the rec room. The place was buzzing. Most of the chairs were filled, and the games tables were surrounded by people. She spotted her security team sharing some homebrewed beers around a small table. Miles nudged her forward, and she got nods and hellos. Someone shoved a beer bottle into her hand.

She listened to the flow of conversation. She had a good team. They were dedicated and hardworking. Several were older, experienced hands like Miles, and others were young, fresh, and keen. Suddenly, wild laughter broke out across the room and she glanced over at the source.

Her gaze fell on the berserkers.

The men of Squad Three were all big, tattooed, and covered in beards or scruff. A year ago, they would have set her teeth on edge. She was well-aware they were wild and unruly, as most of them were former mercenaries, bikers, or criminals.

She spotted Manu with them and her muscles locked. He was hard to miss. He stood a few inches taller than the rest of the berserkers. He was talking with the dark-haired Dom Santora—a man who made every instinct in Kate go on high alert. She'd heard dark whispers about the man and his questionable past. Manu laughed then, and turned to elbow his brother, Hemi. Tane was nearby, as well, and taking the trio in all at once, there was no missing the fact that the three of them were brothers.

All of a sudden, Manu's head shifted and his gaze locked with hers.

She held those dark eyes for a second, before she looked back at her team.

Miles and a younger former soldier, Brandon, were deep in a hot discussion about the Gizzida, and the black octagon device that the berserkers had spotted on a previous mission. Rumors were running rife throughout the Enclave as to what possible horror the aliens were cooking up next.

Everyone knew the aliens were working on some mysterious weapon to wipe out the last of humanity. What they didn't know, though, was if the octagon was that weapon or not. She let them talk, listening and absorbing, not joining in. Suddenly, she noticed that everyone's drinks were getting low.

"I'll grab another round," she said.

At the self-service bar, Kate set the empties in the recycling box, and opened the fridge to grab some fresh homebrews. Two big hands gripped the bar on either side of her, caging her in.

She stared at the bronze, brawny arms for a long moment, before she turned her head. "Rahia."

"Captain." He had an unreadable look on his face.

"There a reason you have me blocked in?"

"Wanted to talk."

When he didn't say anything else, Kate fought the unfamiliar urge to fidget. "I got the carbine." *That's it, Kate, be polite and professional.* "Thank you."

"My job. Can't see what caused the problem, but it's fixed for now."

She turned, gaze falling to the black cotton stretched over his enormous muscles. He still didn't back off.

His lips quirked. "I've been watching you for months. You're always so cool, but I liked seeing you get fired up about the carbines. You should lose your cool more often."

Damn, she was just glad he thought it was solely about the carbines. She dragged in a deep breath and smelled him. Musk and man. She cleared her throat. "It's not my job to lose my temper."

"You're not always on the clock." A pause. "I'm still running some diagnostics on the carbines. Don't like the fact that two went at the same time."

She nodded. "I'm sure you'll sort it out." She ducked under one of his arms and slid sideways, trying to escape. When he moved with her, a hint of panic spurted in her veins.

If the man didn't back up, she'd embarrass them both by doing something very un-Kate-like. Like tear his clothes off and lick his skin. Or climb his big body and rub against him.

Distraction. She needed a distraction. "So, you were out on a mission today."

He was silent for a beat. "Yeah. Drones picked up some strange alien activity in the mountains. Looks like they exploded something. Probably a test."

Damn. Her interest sharpened. "Something to do with the octagon?"

"Couldn't tell. I'm examining the debris."

They lapsed into silence again. She got another deep breath of male mixed with soap and she locked down her body's response. She needed to get away from him.

"Heard you put your team through their paces in the gym today," he said.

She looked up at him. "Where did you hear that?"

"Oh, I've heard all about Captain Scott's rigorous, torturous training sessions."

She straightened. "They need to be prepared. I train them just as hard as the squad soldiers."

He nodded. "Good."

His simple praise made her feel warm inside. "I will *never* lose a team member because they didn't have the skills they needed."

Manu tilted his head. "You lost people in the past."

He hadn't phrased it like a question. Her throat tightened.

He lifted a hand, touching her hair. "I was a mercenary for a decade. Saw lots of shit and lost some good soldiers. People who should have gone back to their families to hug their kids, instead, they went home in a box."

He understood. She swallowed. "I had a mission go bad." God, it hurt to think of those kids. And they had been kids, most not even out of their teens.

His big, blunt fingers brushed her cheek now and she shivered. She had to get away from him. She looked around the room desperately and spotted a blonde head.

"Oh, I see Liberty. I need to talk to her. Thanks again." Gripping the glass bottles, she arrowed across the room. "Liberty."

The blonde bombshell turned and smiled. Her hair was loose, styled in gorgeous waves, and she wore a strawberry-red dress that somehow looked sexy and sweet. "Hi, Kate."

As always, Kate tried to work out how this sexy, lush woman had ended up with General Adam Holmes. The man was the perfect example of a controlled military man, with an aristocratic edge. As head of the Enclave, he and Niko were the top-ranking leaders in the base. Adam and Liberty seemed like polar opposites, but from everything she'd seen, the couple were happy and in love.

Again, Kate felt a flash of something that could only be envy.

Liberty pressed a hand to her belly, and Kate remembered that the woman was pregnant. The image of the general cradling a baby tried to form in her head, but she couldn't quite picture it.

"I wanted to ask if..." Kate swallowed, heat filling her cheeks. Liberty ran an underground market on beauty products, toiletries, and other necessities in the Enclave. Shampoo, moisturizer, condoms...and other things. Whatever someone needed, Liberty could usually find it.

The blonde woman nodded, her smile encouraging.

God, this was harder than Kate had imagined. "Never mind."

Liberty grabbed her arm. "Talk to me. Do you need condoms? The doc has short-term contraceptive implants working now, so the demand has dropped. I have plenty."

Kate sensed Manu was still watching her from across the room. She felt his gaze on her back like a touch. "No. I'm...not seeing anyone." She sucked in a breath. "That's kind of the problem."

Liberty's smile grew wider and knowing. "Hmm, self-induced relief not cutting it?"

"Ah..."

The woman nodded. "And I know it's hard being the boss." The woman turned her head, something soft flowing over her face. Kate saw the woman was looking at Holmes. "Add in being a strong, experienced female, and it gets hard in a place like this to find...the right company." Liberty winked. "I know exactly what you need."

Embarrassed relief filled Kate. "Thanks."

"I'll take care of it." Liberty patted her shoulder. "I'll be in touch soon."

Kate delivered the drinks to her team. This time, she made an effort to join the conversation. Music started up in one corner, and she spotted Cruz from Hell Squad playing a guitar. His wife and two daughters sat nearby, watching.

Soon, people started breaking away to dance or play pool. She decided it would be okay to sneak out now while Miles wasn't looking. She edged away from her team. She'd taken three steps when a big body stepped in front of her and blocked her way. She bumped into a hard chest.

"Leaving?"

She looked up at Manu. God, she couldn't catch a break. Her skin prickled and her fingers curled into her palms. They wanted to touch. They wanted to know what he felt like.

Desire curled in her belly, low and insistent. *Why? Why couldn't she get a grip on this?*

"Kate."

That deep rumble worked its way through her, and she forced herself not to reach for him. What she needed was to get out of there, fast, and put some distance, and preferably a few concrete walls, between her and Manu Rahia.

WARY BLUE EYES stared up at Manu. Kate was watching him and there was something moving behind her gaze that he couldn't quite read.

Damn, this woman was proving a fascinating puzzle. He was certain most people merely glanced at her composed demeanor and made assumptions. He sure had. But with every interaction, he glimpsed hints of the woman she kept hidden under the captain.

He heard Hemi's laughter echo from across the room and Manu glanced over. His squad was laughing and partying, and several women were hanging with the single guys, faces lined with flirty smiles.

That's usually what he liked—smiles, humor, easy charm.

None of which described Kate Scott. He looked back at her. Fuck, she smelled good, and he knew she wasn't wearing any perfume, it was just her.

"I've got work to do." She skirted around him and headed out of the rec room.

Manu followed her. "You're off duty."

"I still have work to do. Security is twenty-four seven." She lengthened her stride.

"That's why you have a team."

Her eyes sparked. "And I'm their leader."

He smiled. "You can't delegate. Figures."

Her shoulders stiffened. "I delegate."

"You're a control freak."

She stopped and took a step closer to him. "I take my job seriously."

Why was he riling her? Maybe because he wanted to see that flare of passion he'd seen in her earlier. Maybe because he was dying to see what she kept hidden.

"Which is admirable." He reached out, touching the swing of her hair. "But you need some downtime too, Kate."

"I work out. You've seen me at the range."

He shook his head. "That's still work. It's important to remember why we're fighting."

Again, he saw something move through her eyes. "Did you lose someone?"

Her brow creased. "What?"

"In the invasion. Did you lose a husband, a lover?"

Her face smoothed out. "No. Only my career."

"That's not what I meant." He stroked his fingers down her arm. He felt toned muscle beneath her shirt.

"I didn't have anyone to lose." She tried to tug her arm from his. "Stop touching me."

He didn't release her arm. "I like touching you."

Blue eyes met his, something unreadable moving through them.

Suddenly, husky feminine laughter echoed ahead in the tunnel, followed by a man's deep groan. They both swiveled and Manu spotted Levi's tattooed body. He had a curvy redhead pressed up against the side of the corridor. Chrissy's legs were wrapped around her lover's hips, her head tipped back as he kissed her neck.

Manu stifled a chuckle. If the two of them weren't arguing—and they argued a lot—they were going at each other in a completely different way. This was a couple who sucked the marrow out of life.

He looked down and found himself riveted by Kate. She was staring at the couple like she couldn't look away. Her face was tinged with color, her lips parted.

Levi sank a hand in Chrissy's hair, his mouth taking hers. Chrissy undulated against him.

"Kate," Manu murmured quietly.

She looked up and the heat in her gaze made his gut clench. Then he watched as she locked it down. She blinked and her gaze was as cool as a lake. "I have to go."

Manu tightened his hold on her and raised his voice. "Hey, King, get a room."

Levi didn't even look his way, just shot Manu a finger. Then the man hefted his woman up over his shoulder and strode off. Chrissy laughed.

Kate stared after the couple.

"You like to watch?" Manu asked.

Her eyes widened. "What? No!"

"But you're turned on."

Her lips pressed together. "No. I'm not...I don't..." She dragged in a breath. "I'm not the wild, passionate sort. I'm not into exhibitionism or voyeurism."

He leaned closer. "You're aroused, Kate. I can see it in your face. Did you imagine yourself in Chrissy's position? Being touched, kissed, loved?"

A shudder ran through her. "Manu."

Now he heard something he'd never, ever heard in Kate's voice. Nerves mixed with heat. Wasn't that interesting? "I like it when you say my name like that."

"Stop."

"You imagine me pressing you into the wall? My mouth on your skin?"

"This isn't me." She straightened. "I'm not some party girl. You want company, go back to your friends." She started to turn.

He grabbed her other arm. "You have no idea what I want."

He saw her chest hitch and the faintest blush of color stain her cheeks. "I could make you let me go. It'll hurt you more than it hurts me."

Manu smiled. "I know, but I don't think you want me to stop touching you." He reached up, running a finger down the side of her neck. "I'm starting to wonder what it is you want, Captain Scott."

Her eyes closed. "Don't."

"If this alien invasion has taught us anything, it's that life's too short. If you want something, you go after it."

She turned her head away, staring at the wall. "I like to analyze, assess, and weigh the risks. I don't just go after anything."

"Sometimes the risk is worth it."

Her eyes cut back to him now and they were strangely blank. "Sometimes risks are dangerous."

They stared at each other, the air between them thick and charged. Then there was a faint vibration under their feet.

Manu lifted his head and frowned. He saw a matching frown on Kate's face.

"What was that?" she said.

"I felt it too." Grabbing her hand, he pulled her back toward the rec room. Through the door, he saw that most people were still drinking and partying, not sensing anything.

But the berserkers had gone still, all of them trading glances. Suddenly, Kate's communicator beeped.

She yanked the device out of her pocket. "Scott."

"Captain." It was one of her team's voice that came through the speaker. Fast and urgent. "Felipe and Kendra are out on patrol."

"And?" Kate urged.

"There was an explosion. They set something off." A harsh expulsion of air. "It's bad."

Kate's face cooled, turning to stone. "I'm on my way."

CHAPTER FOUR

F ocused, Kate jogged down the hall, ignoring Manu as he ran beside her.

She hurried toward the Command Center and, as the glass doors opened, she rushed through. Bypassing the main area where the comms officers and the drone pilots worked, she shoved her palms against the door to the security office. It slammed open.

"Status," she demanded.

Her on-duty team was sitting at a row of comps. A grizzled, older man, Rob, glanced at her, face grim. "Felipe triggered something."

"Earpiece." Kate held her hand out.

"The camera closest to the explosion was taken out," a woman, Genie, said. Her face was deathly pale as she handed an earpiece to Kate.

Kate quickly shoved the device in her ear. Screams of pain echoed across the comm line. Her body tensed and she gritted her teeth.

She felt a brush of fingers at her lower back, and shot Manu a look before she looked back at her team. "Any sign of alien activity?"

Genie shook her head. "I have the drone team on the line. They haven't detected anything."

Thank God for small favors. "Rob, you're with me. Everyone else, initiate preliminary lockdown procedures. Genie, I need a squad for backup."

The woman cleared her throat. "The berserkers are on call."

"Round them up." More screams came through the comm line. Kate wasn't waiting. "Get Doc Emerson and her team on standby as well."

Kate shot through the door. She knew it took three minutes to get to the Security Team locker room. It was right beside the squad locker rooms, where everyone kept their armor and weapons.

Wasting no time, she hurried down the corridor, rounded a corner and slammed into the room. She yanked open her locker and pulled out her carbon fiber vest.

She was going to rescue her people. They were *her* team. Her responsibility.

She slammed the armor in place and then grabbed a carbine, checking it over. She also attached two small boxes to her belt. The tiny devices that contained iono-stretchers to carry any injured.

A muscled, brown arm reached past her and grabbed another carbine out of the locker.

She swiveled to look up at Manu. "You aren't coming."

"I am." He checked the weapon over with practiced ease.

"You're not."

He raised a brow. "Who's gonna stop me?"

Kate slammed her locker with more force than necessary. "I don't have time for this."

"Ready, Captain?" Rob stepped into view, geared up and holding his weapon. He'd had his gear in the security office.

With a nod, she pushed out of the locker room. The three of them were silent as they walked toward the entrance closest to the explosion point.

At the door, she nodded, and Rob spun the lock. Kate went first, stepping out into the night air.

She scanned the shadows. The moon was out, casting everything in a silver glow. "Genie, any alien activity?"

"Negative, Captain."

Gripping her carbine, Kate went to find her people. For a second, memories returned of that horrible mission when her team had come under fire in the Middle East. They'd been taking aid into a war-torn area. She'd protested taking the young, green soldiers on the mission and had been overruled. She sucked in a breath. She'd lost three good people that day. Not one of them older than twenty-three.

Kate shoved away the thoughts and focused on her surroundings. She'd almost forgotten that Manu was with her; the man moved like a ghost. He was completely at ease with his big body, and there was no hint of the fact that he had a prosthetic leg.

"Approaching location." Every muscle in her body was tense, and she strained to hear any sound.

There were no screams now. No movement.

Then she heard a whimper.

Kate rounded some rocks, and the moonlight illuminated a large, blackened crater in the ground. Her steps faltered. *Hell.*

"Fuck," Rob muttered.

The hardened marine clearly liked this even less than Kate. She felt Manu press close to her back. She hated to admit it, but the heat of him steadied her.

"Felipe?" she called out quietly. "Kendra?"

"Captain." A choked voice riddled with pain.

She moved toward the sound of Felipe's voice and spotted him. He was sitting up, his face covered in burns and blood.

Shit. Shit. Shit. Her stomach turned over, but she moved to him quickly. "We're here, Felipe."

"Check Kendra," Felipe whispered. "She hasn't moved."

Kate swiveled and saw the young woman a few meters away. She was lying on her side, her blonde hair tangled over her face. She wasn't moving.

Manu moved quickly, kneeling beside Kendra and pressing his fingers to her throat. "Alive. Unconscious."

Nearby, Rob stayed alert and on guard.

"It was some sort of fucking landmine." Felipe's body was shaking uncontrollably. "We just stepped through the grass and I heard a beep—"

"Take it easy." Kate eased him back, checking him over. God, he had to be in terrible pain. She took out one of the iono-stretchers and activated it. "I need some help."

Manu was there in an instant, carrying Kendra in his arms. He set the woman down on the stretcher, and then turned to help her with Felipe.

Kate opened the second stretcher and Manu lifted him. Felipe groaned in pain.

Moving to Kendra, Kate touched the woman's pale face. She was so still, all that energy of hers muted. Anger churned through Kate's belly. "Rob?"

"Area looks clear, Captain."

"The area is clear," a dark voice said from the shadows.

Kate lifted her head and saw Tane melt out of the darkness. A second later, the rest of the berserkers appeared like wraiths.

Tattooed, badass wraiths.

They were all armored up, holding their carbines at the ready, faces grim.

"Rob, I need you to take Felipe and Kendra in," Kate ordered. "Doc Emerson and her team are waiting."

The man nodded. Tane lifted a hand, and Levi and Ash peeled off from the squad to help Rob.

Kate looked at her boots, trying to control her churning gut. She was angry. More than angry. Furious. She turned to face the crater.

"Kate."

She tried to drown out Manu's voice. She didn't need sympathy right now, not when she was so close to breaking.

"Need to work out what the hell happened," she said between gritted teeth.

A big hand clamped down on her shoulder. "Your people are going to be okay."

She stayed stiff and still. Then she felt his fingers brush against her neck in the tiniest caress. She closed her eyes for a second.

Don't give in. Don't lean.

She stepped away, clicked on the flashlight on her carbine, and crouched by the crater.

MANU FELT the tension pumping off Kate. He knew how it felt when one of your team was down. Hell, he knew what it felt like to be the one who was down.

He watched as she shut down her reaction and he frowned. He suspected she always kept her emotions tightly secured. She never opened up, and she had no one to lean on.

He knew about keeping shit bottled up. He blew out a breath, well aware he wasn't the best at opening up, either. But he had his brothers and his friends. A few nightmares about losing his leg were nothing. As far as he could see, Kate had no one.

"Fuck, whatever the hell blew up made a mess," Hemi said.

The remaining berserkers gathered around the crater.

"Well, it was definitely some sort of explosive." She touched her ear. "Genie, can you get the drone team to scan the crater for active explosives?"

"Already done," the woman answered. "All clear."

Kate took a step down onto the sloping side of the crater.

"Kate—" Manu growled.

She ignored him, sliding down to the bottom of the hole.

Shit. Without pausing, Manu followed her. His leg did not love the uneven ground, but he ignored the flare of pain.

It was about two meters deep. At the bottom, she crouched, studying the melted mass in the center. It was a black, twisted heap. He frowned at it, aiming his flash-light directly at it.

"Gizzida?" she mused.

"Probably."

She used the end of her carbine to poke at it. Part of the melted mass fell away and some of the unburned parts of the device came into view. Bone, scales, and sinew.

Kate's face hardened. "Gizzida."

It was definitely the aliens' type of tech—mixed with organic components. Dark memories stirred in Manu's head. Memories of another alien device—vicious teeth clamping down on his leg. Searing, stomach-churning pain, and his own hoarse screams.

"How the fuck did they get it so close to the Enclave?" Tane bit out from above.

Manu blinked. Sweat had beaded on his forehead and he saw Kate was watching him curiously.

"There was no way they could have waltzed up here without us seeing them," Hemi added.

Kate raised her head. "That's something I intend to find out."

Suddenly, red lights blinked on in the charred remains. Manu and Kate both froze.

"Captain?" Genie's panicked voice. "Active explosives in your location!"

"Manu, out," Tane ordered.

"Fuck, my carbine just died," Dom called out.

"The bomb's too close to the base," Manu said. "We need to defuse it. You guys back up to a safe distance."

Tane made a growling sound. "No."

"Tane."

"Fuck," Manu's brother bit out. "Berserkers, back up."

Manu yanked his small toolkit off his belt. He never went anywhere without it. "Get out, Kate."

"I'm head of base security, not you."

"Kate—"

She lifted her carbine, aiming the flashlight at the landmine. "I'm staying."

Manu studied the stubborn line of her jaw. Damned if it didn't look attractive, even when he was pissed at her. *Fuck.* He didn't want her in the line of fire.

"You'd better get to work," she said calmly.

He bent over the bomb. "I hate stubborn women."

"I'm real upset about that." Her voice was dry. "You know what you're doing?"

"A little late to ask that now." He pulled out his auto-driver tool. "I know enough. I play with Gizzida weapons for fun."

"You need to get out more," she said.

"Pot. Kettle."

She snorted, but he knew she was hyperalert. He opened up a bone-like panel on the unburned part of the device. Orange goo oozed out. There were organic-looking wires inside.

He poked his tool inside and started fishing around.

"Don't blow us up," Kate said.

"Not on my agenda for tonight." He spotted the wire he knew that he needed to cut. It pulsed gently. "This is it."

Kate crouched beside him, her face tense. She sucked in a deep breath. "Do it."

Manu looked up, his gaze tracing over her face. He reached out and gripped her hair. "Just in case I've got this wrong." He pulled her in until those sexy lips of hers met his.

He meant for it to be a quick kiss, but she made a hungry, little sound and kissed him back.

Shit. For a few shining seconds, Manu forgot about everything except the taste of Kate Scott. Her tongue stroked his and a groan vibrated through him.

The alien device made a beeping sound and Manu pulled back.

Kate cleared her throat. "Better defuse that bomb, Rahia."

Damn. The taste of her was still on his lips and he wanted more. There was heat in Kate Scott—brilliant, scorching heat—and he wanted to be burned by it. She'd been holding out on him.

But right now, he needed to keep them alive.

Their gazes locked, and then he cut down on the wire.

The lights went out on the bomb.

Kate released a shaky breath. Adrenaline surged through him and Manu stood. He ignored the twinge in his leg and leaned over, hands pressed to his thighs. "Fuck."

Then suddenly, Kate moved. She stepped in front of him, grabbed his shoulders, went up on her toes, and slammed her mouth against his.

Manu grabbed her, pulling her closer. He slid his tongue into her mouth and stopped thinking. Damn, she kissed him like he was going into battle and might never return. It was the hungriest, neediest kiss he'd ever had. And he wanted more.

Kate stumbled back, her eyes wide and breathing fast. "Ah, I'll arrange for my team to clean up the area."

So, the captain was just going to ignore the kiss? "I need the parts. Want to study them and see exactly what we're dealing with."

She nodded. "You'll have them."

"Kate."

"Adrenaline. Just glad we're still alive." She turned and scrambled back up the side of the crater. At the top she paused and glanced back over her shoulder. "Good work, Manu."

She meant disabling the bomb, but damn, he wanted her to mean the kiss.

CHAPTER FIVE

For the next few hours, Kate did what she always did, and focused on her job. She directed her team and supervised the collection of the alien device. A grumpy Noah from the tech team arrived, his dark hair disheveled. Clearly, he was unhappy about getting pulled out of his bed. One of his technicians, Marin, was with him.

The cute, curly-haired blonde smiled, and when tattooed Ash reappeared out of the darkness to give her a hard kiss, she smiled even more. The badass and the cute tech geek. Kate shook her head. Apparently, alien invasions made opposites attract.

Noah and Marin got busy with their scanners, crawling over the crater. Kate tried not to let her mind wander. To either her injured team members, or the fact that she'd kissed Manu Rahia. Twice.

Noah slid his scanner away. "It appears safe to bring inside."

"But we brought a strong, explosive-proof box," Marin added. "Just in case."

"Thanks," Kate said. "We'll take it from here."

Rob and Miles worked to get the device loaded, and soon whisked it away. Tiredly, Kate made her way back inside. Her leg muscles trembled and her shoulders ached. She needed some sleep.

But as she headed to the locker room to shed her gear, she felt a warm tremble in her belly. She was deathly afraid that when she finally got to bed, she'd be thinking of a certain big man with hard muscles and dark hair, instead of sleeping. Desire surged, energy zinging along her veins.

Dammit, what was wrong with her? She had injured team members in the infirmary, a shit-ton of work to do because the aliens had planted a bomb practically on her doorstep, and she needed a plan to make sure there weren't more landmines out there.

First things first, she needed to check on Felipe and Kendra. When she reached the infirmary, she nodded at Doc Emerson, who was studying some charts. The lights were low, and Kate spotted Felipe sitting up in his bunk, his face still raw but healing. Kendra was asleep in the bed beside him.

"I gave them both a dose of nanomeds," Emerson said quietly.

Kate knew the tiny medical machines would be hard at work fixing the pair's injuries. "Thanks, Doc."

The woman nodded, her perceptive gaze on Kate. "They're going to be fine."

Kate nodded and made her way to her people.

"I'll be back on duty tomorrow, Captain," Felipe said.

"You have two days off."

The man's face fell. "I'm fine."

"I know. And you'll stay that way. Two days."

He sighed. "Okay."

They talked a bit more, then Kate left him, awkwardly patting his blanket-covered legs. She moved to the sleeping Kendra, and her insides twisted. She looked so damned young. Carefully, so she didn't wake the woman, Kate tucked a strand of Kendra's hair behind her ear.

As Kate headed out of the infirmary, her stomach rumbled, and she realized she was starving. She changed directions and headed toward the kitchen.

"Kate."

The deep voice made her stop and turn around. She saw Roth Masters, head of Squad Nine, striding toward her. His muscular body was clothed in a gray T-shirt and fatigue trousers.

She and Roth had not gotten off to a good start. She'd imprisoned him once, when he'd first arrived at the Enclave. She'd thought he was the enemy, and instead, she'd discovered she'd been protecting the enemy. Funnily enough, she and Roth were now friends.

"You're up late," she said.

"I wanted a status update on this landmine." He stopped beside her. "And to check how you're doing."

She blew out a breath. "I'm fine, but I have two team members in the infirmary. It sucks."

"Sure does." He pressed a hand to her shoulder. "They okay?"

She nodded. "Head injury and burns, but healing up nicely. Felipe is itching to get back to duty."

"You have good, well-trained people, Kate."

"Some of them are just kids, Roth."

"No, they aren't. They might be young, but they are making their choices and fighting for things they believe in."

She knew it was true, but right now, it just made her chest hurt. "Damn Gizzida."

Roth crossed his arms. "Niko and Holmes have a meeting planned for the morning."

She nodded. "I need to work out how the hell the aliens got a bomb so close to the Enclave. And we need to make sure there aren't any more of them out there."

Roth grunted. "We'll get it sorted. You look beat. You need some rest."

"You know how it is, being the boss."

His gaze speared into her. Roth was the kind of man who always got the answers he wanted. "I do. And I know it's important to take some downtime and stay fresh."

Yeah, and he had the beautiful, smart Avery who helped him do that. Kate shoved a hand through her hair. "Yeah. Right."

"Get some sleep."

"I will. Night, Roth. Say hi to Avery."

Kate's stomach was rumbling again and she hurried to the kitchen. It wouldn't be the first time she'd raided the kitchen in the middle of the night.

Inside, she walked through the now-silent and dark dining room. Some bench lighting was on in the neat kitchen, and she made her way to the industrial, stainless steel fridges. She opened one and pulled some things out, setting them on the bench.

Cheese. Bread. Some French onion spread. Olives. She popped a cube of cheese in her mouth.

"I'll have some of that."

She spun, clutching the block of cheddar in her hand.

Manu stood there, showered and changed.

Power emanated off him. He was just so damn masculine and strong. His black T-shirt cut into his big biceps, and her gaze fell to the interesting black ink on his left arm. His legs were encased in tan cargo pants.

Kate felt a flash of heat over her skin and a pulse throbbed between her legs. God, she needed to get a grip on this.

She swallowed and set the cheese down on the bench. She pulled two plates closer, dumped some food on both, then nudged the second plate across at him.

He leaned a hip against the bench and they ate in silence. Strangely enough, it wasn't awkward.

No, awkward would be if she leaped over the bench and jumped him. She choked, an olive catching in her throat. She coughed.

"Okay?" he asked.

She nodded, thumping her chest.

"How are your people?"

"Recovering. Nanomeds are fixing them up."

"That's good."

"Did my guys bring you the alien parts?"

He nodded. "I have a couple of my people sorting

through them. After I grab a few hours' sleep, I'll start analyzing them."

She saw him rub his left thigh. "It hurts?"

He stiffened a little. "Only sometimes. It's tied right into my nerves, so after a long day, I get some pain at the connection site."

He didn't go on and she figured from the tight look on his face that the discussion was closed. Manu had always struck her as adjusting to the loss of his leg and his prosthetic with ease. Looking at him now, tiredness lining his face, she saw shadows in his dark eyes. Now, she wondered if that was the entire truth.

She grabbed a cracker. "If you don't want to talk about your leg, that's fine."

He looked up. "We can talk about the kiss instead."

She froze. "No."

He gave her a slow smile. His smile was gorgeous, his teeth white against his bronze skin. "We need to talk."

His sexy voice rumbled over her. *No, no.* She didn't want to talk. Especially when Manu's dark-velvet gaze was on her, like she was in the cross-hairs of a laser-guided target.

MANU SKIRTED THE BENCH. He saw Kate straighten, and her muscles bunch, readying to move.

He pressed his hands to either side of her hips on the bench, caging her in. But she didn't try to escape. No, Kate Scott had too much courage to make a retreat, even when she wanted to.

51

"Why?" he asked.

She looked up. "Why what?"

"Why not talk about the kiss?"

"Kisses." Her face twisted like she hadn't meant to say that.

He smiled. "Kisses. I'm going to kiss you again, by the way."

She frowned. "No."

Manu tried to hide his smile. Had no one ever flustered the sensible Captain Scott before? "It *is* happening again."

"God, you're bossy. It isn't." Her voice was matter-of-fact. "Neither of us have the time for it."

He smiled. "I'll make the time."

"I have a job to do, keeping the Enclave safe—" She pressed her hands to his chest and pushed.

He didn't budge. "That's not a one-woman job. The squads have lives, Kate. It's important to remember why we're fighting." He reached up and stroked the stubborn line of her jaw.

She did a poor job of hiding her shiver. "This isn't me. I'm not..."

He leaned down, his nose pressed to her cheek. "Not what?"

"Like this. Needy, out of control—"

He pressed his lips to hers. She made a small moan and slid her hands into his hair. Her long body pressed against his and Manu changed the angle of the kiss to go deeper. Damn, she tasted so good.

She moaned into his mouth and Manu cupped her firm ass. He felt her hands slide up under his T-shirt, her short nails biting into his skin. Damn, she was hot. He tugged her closer and felt the edge of her teeth catch his lip. She moaned again.

Then her mouth was on his neck and her hands traveled down to grip his ass. He slid his hands up her body and felt her shiver. She was so damn responsive. Desire was like a battering ram inside him.

"I don't like pushy men." She nipped his neck.

"Then this is going to be really uncomfortable for you."

She looked up at him. "Why are you doing this?"

"Because I want you, Kate. I want to strip you bare, and run my hands and tongue all over you."

Her chest hitched.

"And I want what you're hiding inside."

She shook her head. "I'm not hiding anything."

"I want the fire inside you. That fire you hide from the world."

Her eyes widened. "I'm sensible, practical, and boring."

He snorted out a laugh. "No, you aren't."

Something flared in her eyes. "I am. My ex-fiancé told me. Repeatedly."

Manu frowned. "Then he was an idiot."

She quickly pulled back, shoving against him.

It had been a long day, and Manu was tired and off balance. His prosthetic leg went out from under him and he stumbled. With a curse, he caught the edge of the counter before he embarrassed himself and landed on his ass.

Kate was reaching for him. "Manu, I'm sorry—"

He fought off the mass of uncomfortable emotions that reared up. "Don't touch me."

She froze.

Fuck, he realized how harsh his tone was. But the ugly emotions swelled inside him. Here he was, trying to seduce a woman for the first time since he'd lost his leg, and she got to see him almost topple over like a toddler.

"You don't want to be with a cripple, just say it."

Her head jerked like he'd slapped her. "Don't you put words in my mouth."

Gut still churning, Manu took a step back. He just wanted the blessed darkness and peace of his room. He didn't want this strong woman who he desired looking at him with pity.

"You know what, Kate, just forget it." He pushed off from the bench. "Because you're right, this isn't gonna happen again."

Without looking at her, he walked out of the kitchen, horribly aware that he was limping, and she was watching him.

CHAPTER SIX

K ate motored down the corridor toward the Command Center, sipping her coffee. After her sleepless night, she was going to need a lot of caffeine today. A vague headache pounded at her temples as she headed to the meeting with Niko and Holmes.

She entered the Command Center, nodding at the people manning the desks. The only bright spot this morning was that Kendra and Felipe were being released from the infirmary in a few hours.

Now, she had to deal with the alien landmine situation, and stop herself thinking about Manu.

Apparently, she couldn't make a single right move with that man. Hell, any man. Her life was a testament to that. Taking another long gulp of coffee, she pushed all thoughts of Manu out of her head and moved toward the conference room.

Through the doorway, she saw Niko standing at the

head of the table. He nodded at her and she stepped inside and spotted General Holmes.

And Manu.

His face looked like granite as he gave her a brief, impersonal nod.

"Morning," Kate managed.

"Take a seat, Kate," Niko said. "How are your people?"

Kate sat, watching as Niko and Manu did the same. "They're being released from the infirmary today. I've given them both a couple of days off to rest."

Holmes stood, his hands clasped behind his back. As always, his posture was perfect. The man radiated authority. "Let's talk about this bomb. Manu's been analyzing the remains, along with the debris Squad Three brought back from the mountains, so I asked him to join us."

Manu leaned back in his chair. "It's more of a land-mine. I don't have a lot to tell you yet. I need more time."

Kate fiddled with her coffee cup. Did the man's presence have to take up the entire room? She did not like the fact that he wasn't really looking at her. He was sort of looking through her, and dammit, it hurt. All because of that ill-advised encounter in the kitchen.

"How could they possibly have planted it so close to the Enclave?" Niko's voice snapped Kate out of her thoughts.

"The drones didn't detect any aliens close to the base," Kate said. "So, the answer is...I don't know yet." The image of Felipe's burned face flashed in her head. "But I'm going to find out."

Holmes nodded. "We also need to scan all the area surrounding the Enclave. We have to make sure that there are no more of these devices."

"Yes, sir," she said. "I'm already putting plans in place for a search. It'll take time."

The general's handsome face turned considering. "I have all the squads busy at the moment. Those not on security patrol are working to discover where the aliens have moved the black octagon device."

Kate fought back a cold shiver. The octagon device was a priority. The Gizzida had gone to great lengths to keep it hidden, and she knew it was vital they find it and figure out what it was designed to do.

"And Noah's team is busy as well," Holmes said. "Working with Emerson, they've had some break-throughs isolating what in the trees affects the Gizzida."

She blinked. That was great news. "Really?"

The general nodded. "It's actually eucalyptus trees that affect the raptors. Or more specifically, the active ingredient in eucalyptus oil. It's called cineole."

Manu leaned forward. "Noah's had me configuring some grenades to hold the cineole oil. Might have some working grenades to test soon."

"Kate, you're down two people," Niko said. "And I already know you've doubled-up on base security since last night."

She nodded again. "It's okay, I'll—"

Niko held up a hand. "Manu and his team will assist you with the landmine search."

Her gut cramped. *Great.* "If you think that's best. I'll get to work."

She gave them a nod and stood. She made a beeline for her office. As she entered the security room, her team looked up, took one look at her face, and got busy with their work again. Damn, she needed more coffee.

In her office, she'd just circled her desk when Manu appeared in the doorway. She stood there, feeling stiff and awkward. "I can do this search by myself—"

"You need help," he said.

Kate released a breath. "Fine. I'm going to mark out a search grid. Once it's done, I'll send it through to you."

"I've got my guys working with the tech team. We're trying to rig up a scanner to detect the materials used in the landmine."

He was keeping this businesslike, so she could do the same. A part of her—a deep, buried part of her—felt a burning flash of disappointment. But this was for the best. "That makes sense. The drones didn't detect this thing, so it's clearly something different, or it was buried too deep in the ground for the drones to pick up."

He gave a brisk nod. "We're working to make sure the new scanner can penetrate far enough."

"Great. So, let's meet in two hours. By then, I'll have the search grid planned, and hopefully you'll have a scanner to test."

"It's a date." Without another word, he pivoted and headed for the door.

Screw this. Kate moved fast, striding past him and blocking the door. A voice in her head was screaming at her to let him go, to leave this alone. But she just couldn't leave it like this, and she wasn't a coward, dammit.

"Don't you ever put words in my mouth again. What

you accused me of last night was something I've never said, let alone thought."

His jaw tightened.

"I've admired the hell out of the way you dealt with your injury. The work you did before was important. But the work you do now is vital to this base. You may not be out there fighting the aliens with your bare hands, but it still counts."

His face hadn't changed. Fine. She'd said her bit.

She straightened and moved out of the way. "I need to get this search sorted out."

She moved to her desk and sat in her chair. She felt his gaze on her, and when she looked up, he was staring at her, his face unreadable.

"You aren't defined by what your damn leg is made of, Manu."

Another beat of silence, then he turned and left.

Kate released a long breath. Damn alpha males. Manu hid his well, under his easy, sexy smiles and competence, but it was there.

Along with the demons that he kept hidden.

———

MANU WALKED through the long grass, swinging the scanner from side to side. It looked like an old-school metal detector.

Kate moved ahead of him, once again in her carbon fiber armor, her gaze alert. She was holding her carbine easily.

Gorgeous. Tough. Strong.

The words she'd said to him in her office had rattled around in his head all morning. He'd fucked up with her. It was clear she didn't let anyone under that armor of hers, and he'd made a small chink. But because of his own shit, he'd screwed up, and he was pretty sure she'd been busy shoring up any weaknesses.

Well, he was just going to have to work hard to get back in.

His ma had always said he was determined when he wanted something—like a boulder rolling down a hill. She said his kind of determined was spelled the same as stubborn.

His ma would like Kate. She'd always appreciated intelligence and maturity.

"Anything?" Kate asked.

"Nope. Nothing on the scans."

Kate nodded. "I hope that means there aren't any others."

"Something tells me we won't be that lucky."

She grunted. "I don't believe in luck anyway."

"So, you were engaged?" Manu asked.

Her blue gaze narrowed on him. "A long time ago."

"Was he Army as well?"

"Firefighter." Her tone was stiff.

Manu's brain created the image of some buff firefighter holding a smiling Kate in his arms. But he remembered what she'd said about him. Manu had already determined the man was a dick. "What happened?"

"It didn't work out." Her tone was as cold as the Arctic.

Manu grunted. "My ma was itching for one of us

boys to get married and give her grandbabies." He felt that familiar grief at the thought of his mother. "We continue to disappoint her."

"My parents were older. And they didn't really care if I married or not."

He frowned. "They must have been proud of your career."

She shrugged. "They owned a deli. They just seemed bemused when I joined the Army."

"And this idiot ex of yours? Was he proud of your work?"

"At first. Until he wasn't."

God, she was buttoned-up tight. Getting anything out of her was like pulling teeth. "Kate—"

She spun, eyes blazing. "He wanted a wife to come home to every night, who'd cook a nice meal and suck his cock when he was in the mood. I worked just as hard as him, I didn't need a second job caring for him, as well."

"That's not what a marriage is supposed to be like."

"He expected me to give up my job, have babies, and play house."

"What happened?"

"Well, he decided a boring, passionless, workaholic wasn't for him. Instead of manning up and telling me how he felt, he knocked up another woman." Her nose wrinkled. "The cute, twenty-year-old daughter of a friend of ours."

Manu grunted. Yep, guy was a clueless dick. "He sounds like a dumb bastard."

"She was a former cheerleader, who giggled non-stop

and spent what I assume was several hours doing her hair and make up every morning."

The guy had cut Kate in more ways than one. Manu knew there were plenty of guys who couldn't handle a strong, competent woman. Luckily, he wasn't one of them. "Sounds to me like you were better off without him."

"That is one thing we can agree on. Now, can we not talk about this anymore?" She crouched, studying a patch of dirt where the grass had died.

"Have dinner with me tonight," Manu blurted out.

Her head jerked up and she shot to her feet. "No."

"I want to apologize for being a dick."

She looked back at him, those blue eyes steady. "It's not necessary."

"It is, but I also want to."

"No."

He moved closer to her. "I know you want to."

Her eyebrows rose. "Did you take up mind reading?"

"No, but I've taken up studying Kate Scott."

Her lips pressed together. "I don't—"

The scanner gave a low beep and they both stiffened.

Kate surveyed the ground. "We're standing on a dead patch of grass."

Frowning, Manu swept the scanner across the dirt. The beeps grew louder and more frequent.

"There was another strange patch of dead grass yesterday," said Kate. "I saw it out on patrol." She lifted her head. "There are a few of them around."

He narrowed his gaze. "There's another one over there. And there."

They moved carefully to another patch of dirt near a small hillock of rocks. They kept their boots on the thick, green grass.

He waved the scanner over the patch of dirt and the device went wild, beeping frantically.

"Fuck."

Anger and concern lined Kate's face. "I'll report in." She lifted her hand to touch her earpiece.

Suddenly, poison splattered the grass nearby. As he heard it sizzle and burn, Manu dropped the scanner and dived toward Kate. She was already dodging, and together they hit the ground and rolled.

"Kate! Manu! Raptors in your area." Indy Bennett's voice shouted through the comm line. She was the berserkers' comms officer and on duty today. "They appeared out of nowhere."

"We see them," Manu answered.

Kate came up on one knee and started firing at the rocks. Manu whipped his carbine off his back, taking aim.

The scaly, reptile-like heads of several raptors were peering carefully over the rocks. The bastards had good cover, while he and Kate were out in the open.

"Cover me," he shouted.

She intensified her laser fire and Manu took off running. He zigzagged, dodging poison spray, and raced closer to the rocks. He yanked a grenade off his belt, activated it, and lobbed it into the cluster of rocks.

Three. Two. One.

Bang.

The grenade went off and guttural shouts filled the air. Several bulky, raptor bodies flew into the air.

"Manu!"

Kate's shout made him spin. He spotted a raptor down on one knee. The bastard was aiming his weapon right at Manu. *Shit*. Manu lifted his carbine...

And saw the laser cartridge die. He pulled the trigger and nothing happened.

Fuck.

Kate sprinted across the grass and dived. She smacked into Manu and they rolled across the ground.

Right behind them, poison sprayed the field, burning holes in the dirt and grass.

Kate rolled off Manu. He yanked out his backup Shockwave pistol and they both came up firing.

"Cover me this time," she said.

She jumped up, breaking into a sprint. She moved like a panther, strong and fast, while he laid down cover fire. Damn, he could watch her run all day.

He kept firing and watched Kate leap onto a large rock. She jumped into the air, legs kicking to take her higher, and she fired on the other side of the rocks. Manu saw raptors fall.

Landing in a crouch, Kate turned to face a final raptor. The alien bared sharp teeth, but Kate fired at close range, and the raptor fell heavily to his knees. With a vicious front kick, she slammed a boot into his chest and drove him backward.

The field was quiet.

Manu rose and walked over. He scanned the raptor bodies. None were moving.

"Nice work, Captain."

She shot him a faint smile.

Suddenly, a soft, skittering noise caught Manu's ear. He moved, lifting his pistol. A small, sinew-like ball circled the rocks. The damn thing had legs. *What the hell?* As it got closer, he saw red lights blinking on it.

"Bomb!" he yelled.

Kate backed away quickly, but the bomb followed her.

She dived and rolled to her feet. The device kept following. "Rahia!"

This time, Manu yanked his shotgun off his back. He aimed at the bomb, but he needed a clear shot. The damn thing was practically between her legs.

"Kate, move!"

"Do it." Her eyes met his, absolute trust in her gaze.

Fuck. He fired and Kate jumped backward.

Boom.

The bomb splattered into goo-covered bits. Kate staggered and fell on her butt, but she bounded back up and ran toward him.

"You okay?" He grabbed her arm.

She nodded.

They turned and scanned the battleground. Manu sucked in a sharp breath. The ruined bomb parts were heating up and turning red.

Shit. Manu tightened his grip on her and dived, pulling her with him. They went down hard in the grass. He covered her body, pinning her to the ground.

Boom.

The blast shot debris, dirt, and grass all over them. He kept Kate pinned down, even though she was struggling to get free.

"Get off me." She shoved at him.

They both sat up. A tiny crater was all that was left behind by the bomb. Kate cursed.

"You're welcome," Manu said.

She elbowed him. "I don't appreciate you jumping on me like I'm some princess in need of a bodyguard."

"Well, it's a nice body, and I have plans for it."

She stared at him for a beat, her gaze narrowing. "In your dreams." She shot to her feet.

He rose, as well. "I've had plenty of those about you, Kate."

Her lips parted, and something moved through her eyes.

But then shouts echoed behind them. He turned his head and saw her security team rushing toward them.

CHAPTER SEVEN

S weaty and covered in dirt, Kate directed her team to dispose of the raptor bodies.

She was pissed. She circled the rocks where the raptors had been hiding. How the hell had they snuck up so close without detection?

What she saw didn't make her very happy.

Manu stepped up beside her. "Dammit."

There was a large depression in the earth. "They came out of the ground."

"From some sort of tunnel." Manu was scowling. "Looks like it's collapsed, now."

"I need to update Niko and the general."

"I'm coming with you. My carbine failed right in the middle of the damn fight. The raptors have something that can disrupt our weapons."

Kate bit off a curse and nodded. "That's what happened to Kendra and me. Let me warn my team, first." She didn't want them out here with the chance their carbines would die on them. "You think it's the landmines?"

"Probably. I need to investigate." His face was grim. "Tell your team to grab some non-laser weapons from the armory. Shotguns, grenades, projectile weapons, crossbows."

Kate nodded. When she finally made it back into the Enclave and walked into the Command Center, she was desperate for a shower. She plucked a few blades of grass out of her hair. She knew if she shook her head, dirt would fall out.

"Kate." Holmes appeared. "Are you two okay?"

She nodded and caught the general's laser-blue gaze, then looked at Niko. "They came out of the ground."

"What?" Niko frowned.

"Tunnels," Manu said. "The one we saw was collapsed, so we can't follow it, but it didn't look big."

"There is no way to tell what kind of network they have down there, but I'm guessing that's what they used to plant the landmines." Kate set her hands on her hips. "Plus, these damn mines have legs."

"Legs?" The general's frown deepened.

Manu nodded. "Couldn't tell from the remains of the first bomb. But they are clearly programmable and can move."

"Just great," Niko muttered.

"My team is currently out scanning for more mines with a squad for backup," Kate said. "We've found several more."

"And we have another problem," Manu added. "I think something in the landmines disrupts our laser weapons. Kate's carbine failed on her earlier patrol, and mine did today."

Both men swore ripely.

"This is bad news," Holmes said.

"I've ordered my team to carry some non-laser weapons," Kate said. "You need to warn the squads as well."

"It'll be done," Holmes said, nodding at a hovering assistant.

Kate moved over to the map on the wall, touching the screen to pull up the landmine locations. Feeling heat at her back, she sensed Manu. He reached past her, helping to mark out the rest of the locations surrounding the Enclave.

Then he touched the back of her head.

"Hey." She knocked his hand away.

"You've got a clump of leaves in your hair." He held them up.

She scowled. He was too close. She couldn't keep her body under control when this man was next to her. His dark gaze was on her face.

"This is all just a fucking distraction," Niko barked out.

Kate blinked and stepped back from Manu. "Sorry?"

Niko waved a hand at the screen. "They're trying to keep us busy, scared, and running in circles."

Manu nodded. "And away from finding the octagon."

Holmes set his hands on his hips, his face forbidding. "They want to keep us here in our home base, while they do whatever the hell they're doing with that octagon device."

Kate looked at the map again, the glowing dots taunting her. "Don't bring any of the squads in to deal with this. Keep them out there and focused on the octagon. My team can handle this." She cleared her throat. "And if Manu continues to help, we can come up with a way to defuse these landmines."

Manu smiled. "It'll be my pleasure."

"We also need a way to determine how many tunnels the Gizzida have around the Enclave," Niko said. "I'll talk to Noah. We need to get a mini-drone underground."

Frowning, Kate considered it. "The tunnel we saw was collapsed and small. Barely big enough for a raptor to crawl through. Not sure a mini-drone will have enough space to maneuver."

"Let's see what Noah can do."

"Do it." Holmes nodded. "Keep us updated."

The general and Niko left, but Manu stayed. And was standing way too close to her. Kate fought the urge to fidget. She was *not* a fidgeter.

"I need to shower and change." She turned her head and a fine rain of dirt fell to the carpet. *Ugh*. She swung her carbine up on her shoulder more securely.

"Me too."

"I'll catch you after and we can plan." She quickly skirted around him and left the room.

But she felt his gaze on her.

Keeping her head down, Kate hurried down to the security locker room. This time of day, the locker rooms were empty, with all the squads out on duty looking for the octagon. She glanced at the door to the berserkers' locker room. There was a hand-drawn picture of a muscle-bound, tattooed soldier stomping on a raptor taped to it.

Shaking her head with a wry smile, she quickly entered her locker room and put her carbine away. She methodically stripped off her armor. Her dirty clothes followed, and after grabbing a towel, she headed for the locker room showers. She would have preferred the privacy of her room, but she wanted this dirt and sweat gone, and didn't really want the grime in the bottom of her shower stall.

Several showerheads protruded from the communal shower and she gratefully stepped under the hot water. She pressed a hand to the white tiles, letting the water beat down over her. For a moment, the water at her feet turned brown, but finally ran clean.

Her thoughts drifted, as the water ran over her sensitive skin. She thought of Manu's big body pressing hers into the ground. Of course, he'd risked himself to protect her. She was pretty sure protecting others was stamped into his DNA.

She couldn't believe she'd told him all the gory details of her aborted engagement to Anthony. She tipped her face up to the water. *Stop thinking about Manu.* Quickly, she finished shampooing her hair. If she kept this up, she was going to need a cold shower.

Shutting the water off, she dried herself and put on a fresh T-shirt and cargo pants. As she headed back out of the locker room, she noticed the door to the berserkers' locker room was ajar, and she heard the shower running.

She stilled. She knew the berserkers were out. Her

body instantly went on alert. There was only one person who could be in there.

Walk away, Kate.

Instantly, images filled her head. Of Manu naked, water sluicing over his gorgeous, lickable brown skin. Of big hands stroking soap over hard abs.

It's a nice body and I have plans for it. The rumble of his voice echoed in her head. She stood there, hands curled into fists, every nerve in her body alive. Then, on autopilot, she pushed through the berserkers' locker room door and closed it behind her.

His discarded gear was resting on one of the benches, and the sound of the running shower was louder now. She couldn't stop her feet as she walked closer.

Steam wafted through the shower room, and she saw him in all his naked glory. His wide, muscular back was toward her, both his hands pressed against the tiles. Her gaze dropped to his tight ass. *Sweet Jesus.* She briefly took in the sleek, black prosthetic leg attached to his left thigh. He shifted a little, the muscles in his ass flexing. Her gaze hungrily moved back up his body, sliding over his big arms to the tattoo wrapped around his left bicep.

Her mouth went dry. *Walk away, Kate.*

She didn't think she'd made a noise, but suddenly, he turned his head. He glanced over his shoulder, spearing her with a look.

MANU STARED AT KATE. She stood there, so neat and tidy, with her wet hair brushed back from her face.

She wasn't beautiful, but she was certainly incredibly attractive, and had that lush mouth made for sin. She stared at him like she was frozen in place.

He had a second to worry. He hadn't been with a woman since he'd lost his leg. Apart from his squad mates, he hadn't let anyone see him naked.

But the heat flaming in Kate's eyes put that worry to rest.

"Come here," he growled.

She didn't move.

He forced himself to stay still under the water. She had to make the decision. He might want to grab her and drag her down onto the tiles, but it was her choice.

That didn't mean he wasn't going to encourage her.

"Kate, come here."

He half expected her to spin and walk out, but she took several jerky steps toward him. Desire was an explosion in his gut. Seconds later, she stood only a meter away, steam wafting around them.

"This is crazy," she whispered.

"I don't mind a little crazy." He closed the distance between them and cupped her cheek. Her hands pressed against his bare chest, flexing against his muscles.

"I'm not crazy," she said. "I never have been. I'm sensible, practical—"

He pulled her closer, his lips against hers. "Let's be crazy together."

He kissed her, his back turned so he blocked most of the spray from hitting her. That delicious taste of Kate filled his mouth, and she kissed him back, wild and fierce. Her hands kneaded his chest and he groaned. He slid a hand into her wet hair, tugging her head back, and deepened the kiss.

He needed more. Much more. Her hands roamed over his chest and then he felt her nails raking his nipple. He groaned again and reached up to cup her breasts through the white T-shirt that was now sticking to her skin. She shuddered.

Manu quickly spun, pressing her up against the tiles.

"So sexy." He moved his mouth, nipping at her neck. She writhed against him, yanking his mouth back to hers. This kiss was hard and hot. She lit up for him like no woman ever had. So hot. So sinful.

Some idiot had had the chance to claim this for his own, and he'd tossed her away. Manu wouldn't make that mistake.

He pushed her wet shirt up, staring at her full breasts cupped by her sensible sports bra. He yanked the bra down and watched the spill of plump flesh. Then he pulled one nipple into his mouth, sucking hard.

"Manu." She pressed against him, husky cries coming from her throat.

"I want to hear you say my name just like that when I'm inside you."

His cock felt like it was made of rock. It pulsed against his stomach and wanted inside her. Inside Kate's soft warmth.

But he sure as hell wasn't making their first time a fast, hard fuck in a locker room shower.

Then her fingers drifted down, stroking over his abs. Her hand circled his cock.

Fuck. He groaned. "Kate."

She stroked him, her gaze on him, her sexy lips parted.

Running on instinct, Manu flicked open the buttons on her cargo pants. A second later, he jammed his hand into her panties.

"Yes," she hissed, arching into him.

He had his fingers on her, and stroked slick, swollen flesh. "So damn wet." He looked up and saw color on her cheeks. "Sexy as fuck, Kate, knowing you want me so much."

Stroking her skin, he found the nub of her clit and rubbed. Her body jerked desperately against his.

"Manu."

"That's it, babe. Get there." He kept up his strokes. "Give it to me."

He felt her body tense and he kissed her, swallowing her cries as she came. Her head dropped against his shoulder, her breathing ragged.

His own desire was a knot in his gut. Didn't help that he was still touching her, and her fingers were still wrapped around his cock. He half expected her to run, but her fingers tightened around him and her strokes increased.

His hips canted forward. *Fuck.*

Manu slid his hand down, wrapping his fingers around hers. Together, they worked his cock, and her other hand moved up, stroking down his left thigh. When she touched where his prosthetic joined his skin, his chest hitched.

She kept stroking his cock and his skin. *Shit.* He

flexed into her hand, a guttural groan ripped from his throat.

"Kate, I'm going to come."

In response, she stroked him faster. He felt everything in him tighten, and a second later, he came hard.

His come gushed out of him, splattering his stomach and their joined hands. Damn, for a second, he was worried his legs would go out from underneath him. He turned, pressing Kate to the wall. He let the water wash over their joined hands.

She was panting against him, and his own breathing was uneven.

"So hot, Kate." The shower was the only other sound over their breathing. "I...haven't been with anyone for a long time."

Large blue eyes met his. "Since you lost your leg?"

That was his Kate. Direct and straight to the point. "Yeah."

She licked her kiss-swollen lips, her voice low. "You're sexy as hell, Manu."

Desire flared again. His woman was still hungry and so was he. He growled.

He was just about to pull her closer, when he heard sounds coming from the locker room. Deep voices and laughter. The berserkers were back.

Kate stiffened.

Shit. The last thing Manu needed was for his squad mates to see Kate completely saturated, her cheeks flushed from her orgasm. He quickly buttoned her cargo pants and pulled her shirt down.

They both straightened.

"There's a back door into a maintenance corridor over there." He jerked his head. "Go."

She gave a brief nod, her gaze unreadable.

She took one step away from him, then spun, grabbing Manu close. He sank a hand into her hair and kept the kiss hard but brief.

"Thank you," she murmured.

Then he let her go and she moved fast. A second later, she slipped through the maintenance door and was gone.

Manu dragged in a deep breath and stepped back under the spray. *Holy shit.*

He smiled. Yeah, he'd known Kate was hiding a whole lot of heat, and she'd left him singed. He couldn't wait to get burned again.

CHAPTER EIGHT

Kate kicked the training dummy again, sending it rocking on its heavy base. She spun and kicked again, following that blow with several hard punches.

She stepped back and looked at her team members watching her. The eyes of several were wide.

"Okay, pair up and get to work," she ordered.

She heard a few groans, but her people moved across the mats and started following her training moves. She folded her arms over her chest and watched. They'd been at it in the gym for several hours, and damp hair was stuck to foreheads and sweaty shirts clung to skin.

None of them had dared ask her for a break. Which was fine with Kate. She wanted to stay busy. And keep avoiding a certain former berserker.

Oh, God, what they'd done...

"Captain?"

Brandon's voice made her jolt. He was eyeing her strangely. She cleared her throat. "What?"

"How's this?" He kicked the dummy and followed with the punch combination.

"You're dropping your elbow."

The young man nodded, and tried it again, correcting the move.

She nodded. "Better. But you need to twist a little more into the kick. Come over here." She motioned him over.

She moved in close, demonstrating the kick in slow motion. Her foot ended up at his neck. "Twist more here, and you'll get more power. Then keep that elbow up as you come in for the cross."

His brow knitted as he concentrated. "Okay."

This time she moved quickly—kick, hit, hit. Her last punch slammed into his chest and he staggered back.

"Sorry," Kate said.

"Probably time for us to move onto something else," Miles called out. "You've worn these kids out."

There were groans and protests.

"We're due to go down to the firing range for weapons practice, right?" Kendra said.

Kate pasted on a smile. "Sure. Let's move." She watched Kendra grin. The young woman seemed to have recovered from her head injury just fine.

Her team shuffled over to grab their things. Kate tucked a strand of hair behind her ear. This was one part of the training she'd been avoiding.

As they headed down the ramp to the firing range, everyone was talking about the landmines. The search they'd conducted turned up more. Now, there were ten of the things that needed defusing. At the moment, they were all cordoned off, and she knew that Manu had defused another two today. But defusing them correctly wasn't a quick process.

"Any news on the alien octagon?" Miles asked.

Kate shook her head. "The squads are working overtime to find it."

Quiet rumbles answered her reply. The device had everyone on edge, and the situation with the landmines wasn't helping.

When they entered the firing range, Kate scanned the space. No sign of a tall, bronze-skinned man. She blew out a relieved breath.

"All right," she called out. "Grab your hearing protection and weapons. I want you guys to practice with the crossbows too. Until we sort out how the raptors are disrupting our lasers, we can't rely on them."

They all set up in their lanes and started firing. Kate walked along the line, correcting form where necessary, and giving praise to those who were doing well and improving. She noted that Kendra was a decent shot. With a little bit of practice, she'd be very good. Kate made a mental note to give the young woman some one-on-one training.

"Hey, Captain," Brandon called out. "Why don't you show us your stuff?"

This was followed by hoots and whistles. She was going to refuse, but when she saw everyone grinning and looking happy, she didn't want to disappoint them. With a mock-scowl, she took the carbine from Rob and stepped up to the firing plate.

An electronic target flashed to life at the end of the alley. Releasing a breath, she raised her weapon and fired.

Kate let herself fall into the haze that always engulfed her when she was firing a weapon. The rest of the world melted away, and there was only her and her target.

"Woohoo, boss." Applause and cheers followed her display.

She lowered the carbine and smiled. She'd scored perfectly.

"You should try this."

Manu's deep voice made her spin. He stood right behind her, in his usual uniform of fitted, black T-shirt, and khaki-green cargo pants. He was holding some sort of upgraded carbine with several attachments on it.

She forced herself to look at him. He was just the man who'd given her a screaming orgasm with his fingers, and then she'd returned the favor. "What is it?"

"I call it an elite carbine. It's been enhanced." He stepped closer, and instantly every cell in Kate's body flared to life. "Better targeting and faster firing. It can also be switched to projectile mode."

Which was perfect when they were facing alien land-mines that could kill their laser weapons. She set her carbine down and took the weapon. Turning it over in her hands, she got a feel for it and held it up to look through the scope. "It's a little heavier."

He nodded. "It's loaded with thermo bullets, but still a perfect weight for you. You need a slightly looser and wider grip." He reached around her, adjusting her fingers on the weapon. Kate breathed him in. Pure Manu.

"You smell good, too," he murmured against her ear.

Kate jerked, but forced herself to contain her reaction. No one else would be able to hear him.

"You smell like Kate plus recently-fired weapon," he drawled. "Sexy."

He stepped back and she dragged in a breath, trying to focus on the target.

"Let's see it, Captain," Brandon called out.

She tightened her hold on the elite and fired. Her first shot went wild. As one, her team groaned.

She fired a few more times, adjusting to the feel of the weapon, and ignoring the throb of Manu's presence at her back. Finally, she found her groove and started firing well. She switched to projectile mode. The electronic laser target at the end of the lane slid away, and a paper target appeared. Kate smiled, firing bullets into the raptor-shaped outline.

It was a formidable weapon. Well-balanced and with better targeting. She finally lowered it.

"It's really good." She handed it back to Manu, and watched long, blunt fingers wrap around the metal. Fingers that had stroked her, touched her, brought her to orgasm. *Shit.* "How's the landmine defusing going?" The words came out in a rush.

"We got another two done." He frowned. "Wish I could move faster."

She thought he looked tired. "I'd prefer you didn't blow yourself up trying to go faster."

A faint smile. "Really?"

Aware that her team was watching them, she turned to the group. "Okay, you slackers, show's over. Get back to work."

They moved back into their lanes. Manu turned to watch them, nodding his head. "They look good, Captain."

"Thanks."

He stopped by Brandon, giving the man a few pointers. He continued down the line, taking his time to talk with each one. He had good advice and he shared it well. He wasn't condescending or too critical. She watched him, admiring his skill.

"Okay, dismissed," Kate called out.

"Finally." There were murmurs and laughter as her team gathered their gear.

"Thanks, Captain." Rob gave her a nod. The rest of the team hurried out after him.

Kate turned to leave as well, but strong fingers grabbed her arm. "Leaving so soon?"

She stilled. "Manu." Hell, she had no idea what to say to him. She'd acted like a sex-starved maniac with him.

"Have you eaten?"

She jerked her gaze up to his. "We grabbed a snack during training." Not that she'd eaten much.

"Come sit with me while I eat." He pulled her into his office.

Be an adult, Kate. God, they were both single, consenting adults. Some people around here had sex all the time with different partners. Views on sex had changed after the invasion. It was a way to connect with others, a way to escape the constant pressure of knowing they were all in a vicious fight for survival.

Manu's office was messy. *Huh.* For some reason, she'd

imagined he'd keep everything like the firing range—neat and tidy. But in here, there were piles of paper, books, and manuals.

"You're messy."

He cocked his head, and she thought she saw faint color along his cheekbones. "I know where everything is."

There was a tray of food resting on the edge of his desk. He'd obviously had it delivered from the kitchen. He dropped into a beaten chair and nodded for her to sit in the other chair.

He picked up some buttered bread from the tray and offered it to her. Realizing she was starving, she took it. He grabbed another hunk of bread and popped it in his mouth.

"You've been avoiding me today," he said.

She shrugged. "It seemed like the best thing to do."

His gaze was unwavering. "Why?"

"I was embarrassed."

"About a hot, sexy moment between two consenting adults who want each other?"

"I...lost control."

He leaned closer. "And it was fucking hot. I want more."

She shook her head, panic flaring inside her. This was too crazy. She wanted her sedate, controlled life back. "I'm not like this!"

"Just relax and enjoy it." His sexy smile made tingles start in her belly. "You lit up for me, Kate. It was hot as hell. You were so hungry, like you couldn't get enough, and I know you want more."

Her belly clenched. "God, you make me sound desperate—"

"I never said that." He reached out, playing with strands of her hair. He was so close that they were breathing the same air. She felt the glorious heat pumping off his big body.

"I'm not like this," she said.

"You are with me." His finger traced over her lips. "I want to be deep inside you. I want to fuck you hard and drive you wild."

Flames licked in her belly and she made a growling sound. Then, without thinking, Kate jumped on him.

AS KATE LANDED ON HIM, Manu grunted. She straddled his hips and he put his hands on her ass, pulling her closer. She slammed her mouth down on his.

Damn, she felt good. Solid curves and the sweet smell of woman and carbine.

He deepened the kiss, sliding one hand into her hair so he could get more of her.

Suddenly, a wolf whistle pierced the air.

Fuck. He pulled back and saw Kate suck in a shocked breath.

He looked over his shoulder, and saw his damn brothers standing in the doorway. Hemi was grinning like a fool and Tane's lips were curved in a faint smile.

Kate jumped off Manu's lap, but he yanked her back into her chair. Then he slid her chair right up to his. He wasn't letting her run off again. She shot him a look and huffed out a breath.

"Jesus." She reached over and grabbed his soda, taking a long gulp.

"Well, that was *not* what I thought you were doing down here," Hemi said.

"Can it, brother." Manu's voice was one step above a growl.

His brother laughed.

"Hi, Kate," Tane said.

"Hi." She shifted in her seat. Manu slid his arm across the back of her chair and earned himself a glare. He kind of liked her glares.

"We came down to check on the landmine situation," Tane said.

"It's going fine," Manu answered. "Slower than we'd like, but it's going." He reached over and pushed more food toward Kate.

She pushed the plate back at him. "Look, I need to go. I have patrol with Kendra and Rob."

Manu stood. "Actually, I'm coming with you. I swapped out with Rob. I want to defuse a few more landmines."

Her eyes narrowed, and Manu fought back a smile.

"Should be a fun night," he said.

Hemi laughed again. "You two together...now I see it, it's perfect. Can't wait to tell Cam."

"We are not together," Kate bit out.

"We are," Manu said.

He heard her growl and glanced at his brothers. "Anything on the octagon?"

Smiles morphed into scowls.

"All we know is that the alien bastards moved it from the dome," Tane said.

"The dome you blew up," Kate added.

Hemi grinned. "Yep."

"We have no idea where they've taken it," Tane continued. "Drones have found no sign of it, or any increased alien activity."

Kate frowned, her fingers tapping against her thigh. "They never stop."

"But they've never seen determination like ours," Manu said. "Or ingenuity."

"And they don't understand why we keep fighting, despite the odds," Tane added.

"And they sure as fuck don't understand love," Hemi said. "Speaking of which, I have a sexy woman to get back to." He winked at Kate.

"Be careful out there." Tane's intense gaze moved from Kate to Manu. "Let me know if you need us."

His brothers left, and when he turned to Kate, he knew she was getting ready to bolt. She wasn't looking at him, probably thinking she could go back to ignoring him.

She had so many damn defenses. But Manu was good at sneaking behind enemy lines. Or blowing through them, if needed.

"Can I interest you in a pre-patrol quickie?" he said.

Her head snapped up and she glared at him.

"You're right," Manu said. "We need way more time than that. Hours. Lots of hours."

"Manu—"

"Not letting you ignore me or hide from me anymore, Kate."

Her jaw tightened and she headed for the door. "I need to get ready for patrol."

So damn stubborn. "Kate?"

She paused in the doorway, but didn't look back.

"I have something for you." He grabbed the elite carbine off his desk and walked over to her. He held it out.

She looked up. "Manu—"

"It's yours. I designed it for you. I've watched you down here in the range for so long, and I knew you needed a faster weapon. I know you'll put it to good use."

She took it and he watched her stroke the butt. She looked like women in the past had looked when he'd given them flowers.

"Thank you."

He watched her fingers and wished she was touching him instead. "My pleasure."

"I'll see you for patrol." She shot him one last look before she left.

Manu grinned, watching her perfectly toned ass as she strode away. Yep, her defenses were going down.

CHAPTER NINE

God, she'd made out with Manu in his *office*.

Kate walked quickly back to her room. Clearly, her body had been taken over by an alien presence or she was coming down with a virus. Even now, she was vibrating with need.

When she reached her door, she saw a black box resting on the floor in front of it. Frowning, she scooped it up, eyeing the note attached to it.

Enjoy. - Liberty.

Liberty had signed her name with a loopy flourish.

God. Kate stumbled into her room and closed the door. The lights came on, and she set her new carbine on the table. As she walked to her bed, she opened the box. A very long, very thick vibrator was nestled inside.

A choked laugh escaped her. Well, she'd gotten two pretty unique gifts today. She lifted the vibrator, knowing she needed to get ready for patrol.

But desire was like a hot burn in her veins.

Shaking her head, she dropped the vibrator on her bed and started stripping. She needed to change, get armored up, and then get upstairs to meet Kendra and Manu.

Manu. Big, muscled Manu. Who she'd spend all of patrol walking beside, watching, smelling.

Undecided, Kate stood there in only her bra and panties. Her body trembled and she looked at the vibrator again. She sank onto the bed and picked it up. Turning it on, it pulsated in her hand, near silent.

Licking her lips, she moved it, trailing it down her bare belly. She should be getting dressed...

She moved it between her legs, the sweet vibrations rocketing through her. She closed her eyes and instantly pictured Manu. Imagined him on his knees in front of her, parting her legs, his big calloused hands moving over her body.

The vibrator touched the right spot, pleasure rocketing through her. She needed this. She could be quick.

Thirty minutes later, in her armor and holding her carbine, she met Kendra and Manu at the northern entrance.

"Ready?" she asked, not meeting their gazes.

Kendra nodded, enthusiasm on her face. "Sure am."

"Good." Kate opened the door and waved the woman through.

As Manu brushed past her, he paused, gripping her arm. "You okay?"

Yes, I just had a wonderful orgasm imagining you going down on me. Heat hit her cheeks. "Peachy."

He studied her face, like she was a puzzle to solve. Then he ducked outside.

Outside, Kate kept her new carbine balanced in her arms. Kendra walked beside her, vibrating with energy, and Manu was following behind them. The sun was setting, casting a golden glow over the surroundings.

Manu and Kendra were talking about rugby, which Kendra had apparently played in high school and missed like crazy. Kate listened to the conversation with half an ear, enjoying the rumble of Manu's deep voice.

She was tense. It had nothing to do with the aliens and everything to do with Manu. No one had ever bothered her like he did.

She was going to sleep with him.

The thought made her insides quiver. She couldn't ignore him or avoid him, and dammit, she didn't want to. It was time to woman up and deal with her attraction.

"We're coming up on the next landmine," Kendra said.

Kate turned her head, shining the light on her carbine down at the ground. The patch of dead grass was illuminated in the light.

"Let's get to work." Manu shifted closer, setting down his toolbox.

"We dig from the side here, right?" Kendra pulled out a sonic shovel.

Kate nodded, and the woman started digging. Beside her, Manu opened his toolbox and pulled out his tools.

Soon, Kendra was grunting from the hard work of digging through the compacted earth. Kate took over for a bit, shoveling down deeper.

Manu brushed past her and jumped into the shallow hole. He touched his ear. "Enclave? Anything?"

"Nope." Indy's irreverent voice. "No aliens on scans. All clear, big guy."

Manu gently dug sideways through the dirt. A second later, he uncovered the blinking lights of another alien landmine.

His face set with concentration, Manu put the shovel down, and lifted his other tools.

Kate resisted the urge to tap the toe of her boot on the ground. Nothing like watching someone defuse a bomb to increase your edginess. But as she watched him work, she relaxed a bit. A man like Manu wasn't brash or risky. She knew he could laugh loud and be just as wild as his brothers and fellow berserkers, but he could be intensely focused, as well.

"Kendra, do a perimeter check," Kate ordered.

The woman nodded and stalked off silently into the growing darkness. Kate checked the urge to follow her. She was still feeling edgy and protective after Kendra and Felipe's near miss.

"Let her do her job," Manu said.

Kate huffed out a breath. "Stop reading my mind."

He smiled briefly before focusing back on the mine. The minutes ticked by and as the darkness grew, Kate flicked on her carbine's flashlight.

Finally, Manu straightened. "It's deactivated."

Kate nodded. "Nice work."

"I'm good with my hands," he said.

She snorted.

All of a sudden, a loud, discordant beep cut through

the air. Kate swiveled, lifting her carbine.

"Shit." Kendra's voice from nearby. Kate could just make out her silhouette. "Dammit, I stepped on one!"

"Hold still." Kate kept her voice calm as she pulled out her portable comp screen that showed the map of landmines. She looked at Manu. "This wasn't here a few hours ago."

"God." Kendra's voice was breaking, breath sawing roughly in and out of her chest. "God."

"Stay still, Kendra. We'll get you out."

"Kate, we need a plan," Manu said. "There could be more. Clearly, the aliens planted more of these fucking things after we ran our initial scans."

She didn't care. She was getting her team member out. "I'm not sitting around waiting." She lowered her voice. "We have no idea how long she's got. That damn thing could blow at any time."

She shifted closer to Kendra.

Beep.

Kate froze. Her blood turned to ice. Her gaze lifted to meet Manu's and he uttered a low curse.

"Enclave," Manu said. "I need Squad Three. There are unaccounted for landmines, and Kate and Kendra are standing on two."

Indy cursed. "I'm contacting Tane now."

"Warn them that there are extra landmines out here."

"Oh, God." Kendra's voice was frantic. "What's happening?"

Kate looked over. The ground beneath Kendra's boots was bubbling and starting to liquefy.

"Kendra!" Kate forced herself not to move. She wanted to help, but she was stuck and powerless.

Suddenly, the ground beneath Kate started to liquefy, as well. Like it was turning to boiling mud.

"Kendra, move!" Manu bellowed.

Before Kate could do anything, Manu dove. He hit her hard, lifting her off her feet. They flew through the air. His big body curled around her, and they hit the ground with a heavy, jarring thud.

Boom.

Boom.

Mud sprayed over them, and it was like a replay of the other day. Except this time, the dirt was hot mud. In the chaos, she heard Kendra scream.

"Let me up." Kate struggled against Manu.

He rolled off her and she shot to her feet. Manu rose beside her. They were a few meters from a newly formed crater.

Kendra was doubled over, writhing on the ground nearby, on the edge of a second new crater. She was covered in blood and mud.

Then Kate's gut rolled and nausea rose in her throat. One of Kendra's legs was a mangled mess of flesh and blood.

No. Kate rushed over to her. The woman was breathing fast, her body going into shock.

"Lie down." Kate kept her voice matter-of-fact and helped Kendra down. Kate yanked her field first aid kit out and grabbed a bandage. She tied it around Kendra's thigh to stem the flow of blood.

Manu crouched, his face like stone. He looked pale

under his dark skin. He held up a pressure injector. "Pain killer and clotting agent. Hey, Kendra, got some good drugs for you."

The woman managed a grimace, and Manu touched the injector to her neck.

"We'll take care of you," Kate murmured.

"You always do," Kendra choked out. "No one really sees how dedicated you are. How well you look after your team."

Kate's throat went tight. She stroked Kendra's bloody hair back from her face.

One man saw her. He saw right through her. She glanced at Manu before she took out more gauze and wadded it against Kendra's leg. A second later, the other woman lost consciousness.

Kate sat back on her heels. "God, Manu." She pressed a hand to her eyes.

He leaned down and grabbed her hand. "We'll get her through this. Together."

For the first time in forever, Kate let herself lean on someone else.

MANU MOVED CLOSER TO KATE, feeling the rigidity of her body. She held her injured team member's hand, her gaze on Kendra's face.

She was holding on, but she was on the edge. Worry for the younger woman was stamped all over her features.

Manu looked at the woman. Poor Kendra. He felt his own nightmares shift in his head. He remembered all too well how it felt to be in Kendra's position. He remembered the shock and pain of losing his own leg. His gut churned painfully.

Suddenly, he heard pounding footsteps behind them.

"Incoming," Tane's voice echoed in his ear.

A second later, his brother arrived with the rest of the berserkers. They'd come fast and weren't even wearing full armor.

"Fuck me," Hemi muttered.

"I have a stretcher." Ash stepped forward, opening up the iono-stretcher. "Doc Emerson and her team are waiting."

Kate grabbed Kendra's arm. "You're going to be okay. I'll make sure of it."

Manu gripped Kate's shoulders and pulled her back. He got an even better view of the woman's leg. It was a hell of a mess. Manu tasted bile. She'd lose it for sure.

Manu's dark memories stirred, like a hungry beast waking from hibernation. Ready to shove against the cage that Manu kept them locked in.

Ash and Levi lifted the unconscious woman onto the stretcher. Kate was standing still, so still, her gaze trained on her injured team member.

She stiffened. "What the hell is that?"

Manu saw she was looking at Kendra's damaged leg. He leaned closer to get a better look. There was a strange dark patch on the woman's thigh. *What the hell?*

"They...they look like scales," Manu said.

"It's embedded in her skin." Kate's voice was horrified.

"It must be some sort of debris from the mine,"

Manu said.

"Let's get her to the doc," Tane ordered.

Kate swiveled. "There could be more mines, ones we don't know about."

Shit. Manu looked around. "The ones we stepped on hadn't had time to kill the grass. Just avoiding the dead patches isn't enough."

"I can help with that," a soft voice said.

They all spun and Manu saw Tane stiffen.

A slim woman stood nearby, her dark pants blending into the night, but her pearlescent skin glowing in the darkness. Selena's silver-white hair was pulled back in a ponytail which accented her overlarge green eyes. A large black bird was perched on her shoulder, huge claws curved over her dark shirt.

"What the hell are you doing out here?" Tane barked.

Selena shot him a look, then looked at the injured woman on the stretcher. "The general approved it." There was a faint trace of attitude in her voice.

Manu raised a brow. When the alien woman had first been rescued from the Gizzida, she'd been shy and shell-shocked. She was an enemy of the raptors who'd been abducted from her home world.

Now she was a survivor, far from her own planet, and called the Enclave home. Manu had watched her the last few months and seen her growing stronger.

"I think I can detect the alien landmines," Selena said.

"How?" Manu asked.

Selena crouched. Her pet, Fluffy, fluttered his sleek, leather-like wings then settled again. He was from Selena's world, and had been experimented on by the raptors before he'd been rescued by Finn and Lia.

"I can..." She tilted her head, like she was searching for the right words. "I can detect energies and I can feel the...disturbance caused by the Gizzida technology." She pressed her palms to the grass.

Manu glanced at Kate. She was staring at Selena, curiosity on her face. He looked at Tane again. There was something very different on Tane's face.

Selena's hands glowed and she tipped her face back, her eyes closing. Manu didn't see anything, but he felt a ripple of energy pass over him. The way everyone shifted, he knew the others had felt it too.

When Selena rose, her eyes were glowing bright green, and Fluffy took to the air. She held her hands up in front of her. Around them, the ground vibrated. In a few places nearby, he saw the ground burst upward, dirt flying. Curses erupted and the berserkers swung their weapons around, flashlights illuminating the darkness.

"Holy shit," Kate murmured.

Several landmines moved into the air, then gently lowered onto the grass. Their lights blinked, but they didn't heat up or explode.

"My range isn't large, so don't walk outside of those landmines," Selena said. "But you should have a clear path to the Enclave entrance."

Ash and Levi moved fast, pushing Kendra's stretcher ahead of them.

Tane strode up to Selena, his intense gaze on her face. "Back inside now."

"There are more mines to find—"

He gripped her arm. "Tomorrow, in the daylight, and with a full squad protecting you."

Selena's face took on a stubborn look. "You don't give me orders, Tane Rahia."

He ignored her and started pulling her toward the entrance.

Selena held up a palm. She didn't touch Tane, but he staggered back a step.

His gaze narrowed and his voice lowered. "You think a little shock is going to stop me? You don't know who you're dealing with."

Hemi glanced at Manu, his eyes bugging out of his head. He was doing a piss-poor job of hiding his grin.

Suddenly, Tane gripped Selena's narrow waist and lifted her. He tossed her over his shoulder and started for the entrance.

Tane let out a sharp whistle. "Fluffy."

The bird swooped in and landed on Tane's other broad shoulder, seemingly unconcerned that his mistress was being carted off.

Selena shot a hot glance at her bird. "Traitor."

They disappeared into the darkness.

An interesting interaction for Manu to ponder at a later date. He looked at the other berserkers. They were all grinning and shaking their heads.

"We'll do a quick perimeter check." Hemi signaled to Dom and Griff, and the trio moved off.

When Manu turned back to Kate, he saw she was staring at the blood on her hands.

He touched her shoulder. "Kate?"

"It's my fault."

"It's the Gizzida's fault."

"Kendra's on my team, my responsibility."

"She'll live."

She spun. "She'll lose her leg!"

"But she'll live. She'll survive and she'll adapt. I do it every day, remember?"

Kate's eyes flashed. "I remember. But not everyone's as well-adjusted as you."

Manu fought the urge to laugh. *Well-adjusted.* "I'm not always, but whatever shit life throws at you, you deal and move on. I'll help her. She's tough, and she'll be fine."

Kate stood there, looking so alone. Manu wrapped an arm around her and pulled her in to his chest.

She pressed her face against him and stood there, stiff for a second, before her arms snaked around him. She held on tight.

He felt like he'd won a prize. Kate Scott was leaning on him.

"I should have guessed they'd try something like this." Suddenly, she exploded with anger and yanked away. "God, I hate the aliens. I vowed to protect my team, and they hurt Kendra. Again. Bastards!" Her hands clenched into fists. "I'm going to make them regret this."

He liked seeing her release her emotions rather than lock them away, but the violent edge on her face didn't look healthy. "Kate—"

"I... I need to be alone." She spun and jogged back toward the entrance to the Enclave.

Manu watched her. No, he decided, the last thing she needed was to be alone.

Swinging his carbine onto his shoulder, he followed.

CHAPTER TEN

K ate sat outside the infirmary. She forced herself to sit still, even though everything inside her was a mass of whirling emotion. She forced herself to stay there. Waiting. Waiting.

"Kate?"

Doc Emerson's voice made her glance up and she shot to her feet. "How is she?"

"She's stabilized. I've given her a dose of nanomeds." The doctor's voice was tired.

"And her leg?"

Emerson's smile dissolved. "It was too badly damaged. We amputated just above the knee."

Kate had known it was coming, but God, it was still a blow.

"She's alive and her vitals are stable. We'll work on a prosthetic for her and some therapy. You know Manu and several others here have recovered very well from losing a limb."

Kate managed to nod. But she was also well aware it was still a hard road to recovery. She'd seen the shadows in Manu. The things he refused to talk about.

"Thanks," Kate murmured.

Emerson gave her a nod. "Get some rest, Kate."

Kate turned and headed down the hall, feeling as though a heavy weight had settled on her shoulders. She'd failed Kendra. The kid had been so damn enthusiastic about joining her team. Kate had let her down, and now she'd lost her damn leg.

Kate ran into a hard chest and stumbled to a halt. She lifted her head and focused her gaze. Manu. Of course. She'd thought he'd gone to bed, but she should have known he wouldn't be far away.

"Kendra okay?" he asked.

"Lost her leg."

"Shit," he bit out.

"I'm going to bed." She pushed past him.

He grabbed her arm and pulled her back against his chest. "I know you're hurting. Talk to me."

"Like you talk about losing your leg?"

His face hardened and he remained silent.

Emotions churned inside her, far too close to the surface. "Let me go."

"Never."

She shoved at him, the anger inside igniting. "It's my fault. My fault that she's in that damn bed minus her leg. My fault she almost died. I let her talk me into joining the team. She's a kid."

"Not really. She's a young woman coming-of-age in the middle of an alien invasion. She knew the risks. From what I saw, she was happy to take them. Proud of the work she was doing."

"She didn't know that it would almost get her killed." Kate's words echoed off the walls.

"Sure, she did. She knew. You know. We all know." Manu backed Kate up into the wall. "It's knowing that it's worth it. Knowing that dying is worth it to keep the young and innocent alive, and to give humans a chance to survive. So you can hold your head up high and know you're doing something good and right—" his voice lowered, his lips brushing her cheek "—and it's knowing the people we care about are safe because of the risks we take."

Her gaze dropped to his lips. He was so close, and as always, her body lit up like a damn neon sign.

"She wanted to be a part of protecting what we have," Manu said. "Don't take that away from her."

Kate squeezed her eyes closed.

"Let me in, Kate. Let me hold you and help keep the nightmares at bay."

She opened her eyes. "I don't lean on people." It came out a husky whisper.

"I know. They lean on you." His lips brushed hers. "But I'm right here, babe."

"I don't want to be..."

"Weak? Makes you stronger to hold on in the rough times."

She lifted her hands, her fingers flexing on his wide shoulders. Her gaze dropped to his lips. "I want to forget for a little while."

He groaned softly, and then his lips hit hers. As

always, the kiss instantly turned hot and hurried. She wanted to absorb his strength, so she could stay standing. She wanted to believe she made his risks worth taking.

Manu's big hand grabbed hers and he started down the hall. He was moving so fast she was forced to break into a jog to keep up.

"Manu—"

"Quiet."

He turned them down one of the corridors, heading to the personal quarters. At her door, he stopped. She hit the lock and led him into her room.

A light flicked on, spreading a warm glow over the space. He took a second to scan her space. He smiled. "Neat as a pin."

They turned and faced each other.

"This isn't a good idea," she said.

"It's an excellent idea. You're just afraid."

She lifted her chin. "I am not."

Manu dropped into an overstuffed armchair and spread his long legs. "Prove it."

"I'm not a coward."

"I know that, Kate. Everyone knows that. But you don't have to be superwoman all the time. Here, you can just be Kate."

Things inside her trembled. She spun. "I'm leaving."

She'd barely taken two steps when an arm wrapped around her, just below her breasts. He yanked her back against his hard body, and then his lips were on the side of her neck.

Fire ignited in her skin and arrowed straight between

her legs. She elbowed him, and then she was spinning to face him. They scuffled.

The man was stronger than her.

"I'm not an easy woman, Rahia."

His eyes darkened. "I know."

"I'm tough and used to living my life my own way."

A faint smile. "I can handle you."

She pressed her hands against his chest and shoved hard, knocking him back a step. His legs hit the edge of the bed, and he sat down on it. He looked like a big, dangerous animal sitting there, his gaze locked on her.

"I'm not a very passionate woman, either."

He snorted. "Bullshit."

She frowned. "Well, I haven't been before now."

A wide, white smile unfurled. "So, this is all for me?"

She climbed on top of him. "Don't get cocky." She hesitated. "You sure you can handle me?"

He smiled. "Very sure, Captain. Let's see what you've got."

He rolled, pushing her face down on the covers, and pinning her there. She felt his lips on the back of her neck.

Oh, so good. He found a sensitive spot and she squirmed. She loved his big, hard body against hers.

"Gonna make you scream my name, Kate." His lips moved to her ear, nipping at the sensitive flesh. "So many times, you'll be hoarse tomorrow."

The sexy, dirty words were like an arrow between her thighs. She was drenched. What did he mean, so many times? They were both over forty years old. He wasn't a twenty-year-old anymore. What sort of stamina could he possibly have?

"You have an implant?" he murmured.

She nodded. Pregnancy was a slim option for her, but the implants also controlled disease as well.

She felt his hand slide over her ass and down her hip. It moved under her, and she felt his fingers working at the button and zipper of her trousers.

Then his hand was inside her panties, between her legs, rubbing.

"Oh." She arched.

His fingers rubbed against her. "So wet for me, Captain." He stroked her clit ruthlessly. "Gonna eat you first. Need to taste you."

Oh. God.

His weight lifted off her, and then he pulled her up on her knees. His hands stroked over her ass, sliding her trousers off, and then her panties.

He pulled her back to his chest. His breath was hot on her ear. "Do you know how many times I've imagined you under my mouth?"

She jerked, feeling flames licking at her. No one had ever talked to her like this.

"How many times I've jerked off in my bed, imagining you naked and writhing under me?"

She shoved back against him. "Then put your mouth on me, Rahia."

He pushed her forward onto her hands and knees. His big hands shaped her bare ass, nudging her thighs apart. She felt the bed move, and then she felt his hot breath on her thighs. Everything inside her clenched.

When his mouth hit her flesh, Kate cried out. He started licking her, like he was starving. He gripped her thighs and she heard a growl.

"You're dripping, babe." Then he pulled her back harder against his face. "Taste so fucking good."

His voice vibrated against her and she writhed. He licked and sucked, and small cries ripped from her throat.

"I'll get addicted to this," he said.

She felt a thick finger slide inside and she moaned. He kept licking her, alongside that thick finger stretching her. He pulled it out and two fingers worked back inside her.

"Tight. You'll feel good stretched around my cock, babe."

She pushed back against him. "Manu."

"Sweetest sound, my name on your lips."

Everything inside her felt hot, and her muscles were trembling. Her climax was almost on top of her, threatening like a massive storm.

His fingers thrust deep inside her. His tongue flicked over her clit. "That's it, Kate. Come on my face."

When he sucked again, she screamed and splintered apart. Kate rode through the waves of pleasure, feeling as though she were breaking into pieces.

But Manu's strength held her in place.

MANU'S COCK was so hard it hurt.

He needed to be inside Kate. He needed that more than he needed anything else.

She was collapsed on her belly, panting, but he pulled her hips up and flicked open his trousers.

"Gonna fuck you now, babe."

She pushed against him. "Good."

A straight talker, his Kate. He cupped her ass, and she looked back over her shoulder. Their gazes locked.

He gripped his cock and stroked it. There was raw hunger in those blue eyes of hers. Damn, his woman was wild for him.

He leaned over and gave her a hot kiss, sucking on her bottom lip. She thrust back against him, her tongue sliding to tangle with his.

Then he nudged her legs apart and rubbed his cock against where she was so wet and swollen.

She whimpered and shimmied her hips.

"Hold still," he ordered.

"Inside me," she demanded.

"I'm coming, babe." He started to push inside her.

"Oh, God." Her back arched, and again her gaze found his.

Manu pushed his cock inside her, inch by painstaking inch. He was a big guy, so he knew to take his time. He savored the hot feel of her. So damn tight.

"Oh, my God." Her breath sawed in and out of her chest. Manu pulled back, and then slammed inside her once more, sinking deep and rocking her forward on the bed.

She was stretched tight around him and he'd never felt anything so good.

"Say my name, Kate."

"Manu. God. Move."

He leaned down, pressing a kiss to the center of her spine. Then he started thrusting, hard and rough. He wanted her to feel it. To feel him.

She was making small, sexy cries, each one of them driving him crazy, and he kept up his heavy thrusts. He grasped her shoulders to get more leverage and picked up the pace.

"Best fucking sight in the world, me pumping into you from behind."

She moaned.

Manu wanted to hear her come again, and he could feel his own orgasm barreling down on him. "Touch yourself," he ground out.

Instantly, she lowered her head to the bed and moved a hand beneath her.

"Are you rubbing that sweet clit?"

"Yes."

"You don't come until I tell you."

She stiffened. "Manu—"

He growled "We come together. Hold it."

"I...I can't."

"Keep your sweet ass up, Kate. Take me and hold on."

She lifted her ass. "Manu."

"Nearly there, babe." He leaned over her, sinking his cock inside her as deep as he could. So. Damn. Good. "Come now."

She tensed and her body clamped down on his cock. As he groaned, she screamed, and he sank his teeth into her neck.

She bucked against him, and Manu roared as his release tore through his body. Fuck. *Fuck.*

They collapsed on the bed, and Manu fell to the side, pulling Kate close into him, molding her sweaty body to his. She didn't move, lying completely lax. He buried his face in the curve of her neck.

Manu had been with plenty of women before, but nothing had ever been like this.

He'd also always had something to fight for—his brothers, his friends, innocent kids here in the Enclave.

But now, he had something else. His reward for the fighting and for the loss. A woman who came alive only for him.

A woman he'd happily lose his other leg for in order to keep safe. *His.*

CHAPTER ELEVEN

K ate woke to something bumping into her. The room was dark, and a warm body was pressed against her.

Manu. Manu Rahia was in her bed.

"Fuck, make the pain stop."

His agonized voice cut through the quiet. Her heart clenched. He was having a nightmare.

He thrashed again and she reached for him. "Manu?"

A big arm swung at her and she ducked it. She threw herself on top of him, straddling his chest. She squeezed her knees into his sides. His chest was heaving.

"Manu? It's Kate. Wake up."

He stilled beneath her. She reached over and flicked on the bedside lamp.

They both blinked at the sudden brightness, and Manu watched her with dark, fathomless eyes.

Kate studiously ignored the fact that she was naked. She'd never slept naked in her life. "You with me?"

He nodded. Kate slid off him and tugged the sheet up. He scraped a hand through his hair.

"Is this common?" she asked.

He shrugged a big shoulder. "It happens."

"Have you talked to anyone about it?"

His face turned mutinous. "It's a few nightmares. To be expected."

"Manu, what you went through was tough. There are counselors here at the Enclave—"

"Don't want to talk about it."

"Then talk to me."

A muscle ticked in his jaw. "No."

Hurt arrowed into her heart. "Right. So, it's okay for you to prod at me, but you get to keep all your secrets locked away." She rolled to the side of the bed. "Got it."

He grabbed her, yanking her back onto the bed. "I...I haven't talked about it. Ever."

His voice was raw and full of pain, and her heart clenched. "Your brothers?"

He shook his head. "I've told them bits and pieces."

She cupped his jaw. "I understand not wanting to be weak or show any vulnerabilities. I've made a life of doing that." She released a breath. "I had a mission go wrong. Right before I came to work at the Enclave, just before the alien invasion. I lost three good, bright, young soldiers."

"Ah, that's why what happened to Kendra has hit you so hard," he murmured.

"Losing people is never easy. Just like losing a piece of yourself is never easy." She stroked his jaw. "I talked to the Army therapists. If I hadn't, I think that ball of hurt, rage, and guilt inside me would have grown."

"I don't let it."

"You might keep it locked up, Manu, but it's doing damage."

He pulled in a deep, shuddering breath and was quiet for a long moment. Kate was almost certain she'd lost him.

"We were still at Blue Mountain Base. We were on a recon mission. Just supposed to scout out an area in the city where there'd been increased alien activity."

She stroked his shoulder and stayed quiet. She hated the haunted look on his face.

"Fuck." He took another deep, shuddering breath. "It was a trap. They'd lured us there, and they'd literally set up traps in the ground."

"Traps?"

"Like bear traps. Huge, spiked traps made of bone and metal. We were engaged by a group of raptors, fighting our way out." He shook his head. "Hell, Hemi was laughing. Then I stepped on one of those goddamned traps."

Kate moved, stroking his back.

"The pain was indescribable. I was screaming, the agony was so extreme. More raptors were coming, and I yelled at my squad to leave." Dark eyes met hers, boiling with old horror. "I could see my leg was stuck. The teeth of the trap had cut right through, just above the knee. Blood was pouring everywhere. I kept firing on the raptors. I wanted to hold them off until Tane and the others escaped."

He'd kept fighting. Was thinking of others even when he was so badly hurt. That was Manu. Loyal, protective, and caring.

"They refused to leave me." His voice broke. "They pumped me full of drugs, got me out, and we all kept firing until we made it back to the quadcopter."

He'd survived, but the aliens had still scored a hit and left him with scars.

"You amaze me, Manu Rahia."

He jolted. "Why?"

"You survived a nightmare that would have dragged so many under, and here you are, still doing what you can at the Enclave to keep people safe."

"I still have nightmares, Kate. I still get so damn angry I want to punch things. Sometimes I'm touchy and mouth off."

"No one said you had to be perfect."

He scowled.

"You're the oldest brother, so I guess wanting to be perfect and strong for everyone is a character flaw."

His scowl deepened.

"After everything that happened, you still get up every day and go to work at the range. You are a damn hero, Manu." She cupped his cheeks and made him look at her. "And you never have to hide what you're feeling from me. In here, you can show me when you're hurting or angry."

Manu sucked in a deep breath. "You gonna show me your underbelly, too?"

She wrinkled her nose. "Not much to show. You're

going to wake up one day and realize I'm boring and sensible."

He pushed her back on the bed, covering her with his body and nudging her legs apart. "Never."

God, she loved the feel of him. "You'll see. I'm boring and not sexy, and—" Her words turned to a choked cry as he slid his cock inside her.

He pumped into her, his thrusts relentless. "There is nothing boring about you, Kate. And I'll never get tired of burying my cock inside your hot, sexy body."

Sensations swamped her, every nerve alive. "Manu."

"There it is. I will never, ever get tired of hearing you call out my name just like that." His voice lowered. "Only thing better is when you say it while you're coming."

His words sent her over the edge, and Kate gave him what he wanted.

KATE WOKE with her nose pressed against a wall of hard muscle covered in bronze skin.

She froze. *Oh, God.* Everything they'd done to each other during the night crowded in her head. She shivered. After that mind-blowing first time, they'd looked at each other...and done it again—twice. Then once more, right after his nightmare.

Kate had never had sex like this before.

"Kate." A sexy husky rumble.

"Hey," she murmured.

The arm wrapped around her waist tightened. "Whatever you're thinking, stop it."

She flicked her gaze up to his face. Apart from slumberous, dark eyes, he looked alert. "I'm not—"

"You're freaking out."

"Get out of my head," she muttered.

He reached out, sliding a hand through her hair and pushing it back. Then he pressed a gentle kiss to her lips. "We had sex. Really great sex. Best I've ever had."

She felt the burn of heat injected into her cheeks. "Oh."

He smiled that sexy, white smile of his. "And we're going to do it again. Lots."

"A bit presumptuous."

"Babe, you came alive for me. I've never had a woman so hungry for my cock."

She frowned. "Don't be crude."

"Babe. It was hot."

Kate felt embarrassed. She'd never been like this with a man before. Then again, she'd never been with a man like Manu before.

She quickly moved to get off the bed, but an arm wrapped around her, and tightened under her breasts. His skin was shades darker than hers, and she studied the sexy veins running up his strong forearm.

"Manu, I have to get to work."

"We have over an hour until our shifts start."

She felt him move in behind her. He got on his knees, pulled her back to his chest. She felt the broad head of his cock press against her ass. His hand moved down her body, his fingers spreading over her belly.

Then she felt Manu go still. "My Kate's got a naughty side."

She frowned. "What?" She looked up and saw him looking at her nightstand.

Where the vibrator that Liberty had given her was sitting.

Oh, God. "Um..."

He reached around her and grabbed it. Her belly clenched.

"Show me how you like to use it."

She cleared her throat. "I just got it. I haven't really..." She was an adult. She shouldn't feel like a blushing teen caught by her parents.

"You been feeling the need for some relief lately?" His breath was warm on her neck.

She leaned into him and watched as he stroked the vibrator down the middle of her belly. He flicked it on and then ran it between her thighs. She jerked against him.

He pressed it hard against her clit and she cried out. Then he ran the toy along her slick lips.

"Fuck, I need to see your face." He spun her around and pushed her back on the bed. Then he was pulling her legs apart.

With a focused look on his face, he went back to work, sliding the vibrator against her. Soon she was writhing. It felt so good.

"You are so damn gorgeous," he said.

Kate thought the same about him. Big, beautiful, and all that smooth, brown skin. All of it naked and focused on her.

He moved the vibrator and pressed the thick head of it against her. Her lips parted, her hips lifted.

Manu slowly slid the toy inside her.

She moaned. She felt so full, and she still felt the burn of having had him numerous times during the night. It had been a long time since she'd had sex and she was a bit tender.

"Sore?" he asked.

"A little."

"Want me to stop?"

"Hell, no."

A warm laugh. Manu moved the vibrator slowly, but firmly, inside her. Then his finger slid down her belly and started strumming her clit.

She moaned. "Manu."

"Right here, babe." He increased his tempo. "Damn, could watch you all day."

Kate was getting close, all the sensations in her swirling faster and faster. When he pulled the vibrator out of her, she let out a cry.

"Easy." He threw the toy on the floor and yanked her up. "When you come, it's gonna be on my cock."

Then he shifted to the edge of the bed, his feet flat on the ground and pulled her to straddle his hips. He pushed her down, his cock sliding inside her with a hard thrust.

She cried out, her hands gripping his shoulders.

"Ride me," he ground out, his fingers digging into her hips.

Her body moved of its own accord. Up, down. She needed him. She needed this.

"Look." His voice was guttural.

She followed his gaze down to look where they were

joined. To where he was rubbing her swollen clit and where his cock was lodged deep inside her.

Oh, God. Everything inside her gathered like a storm, contracting to a hard point in her belly. Then the explosion happened, and she came.

As Kate arched her back and cried out, Manu gripped her hips and slammed her down. He groaned out his own release, spilling inside her.

She collapsed against him, cheek pressed to his shoulder. They stayed there, waiting for their heart beats to slow.

Again, she'd just proved that she was hot for him. She wasn't sure whether she should be proud or embarrassed. "I didn't think we were supposed to have sex like this."

He made a rumbling noise she took to mean was a question.

"Sex like we're twenty."

"This is better than sex when you're twenty, impatient, and clueless."

Amen to that. She lifted her head. "I want to see Kendra before we head back out to tackle more landmines." She tried to move off Manu.

He held her still, one big hand stroking her back. "She'll be okay, Kate. We'll see to it."

She peered at those dark, velvet eyes. "You'll talk to her?"

"Shit." Manu pulled in a breath. "Yeah."

Kate could see that talking about losing his leg wasn't going to be easy for him, but that he'd do it. For her.

"It'll be a tough road for Kendra, but she'll make it."

Kate's fingers dug into Manu's skin. "I know now that wasn't as easy as you made it look."

He sighed. "No."

"Will you talk to me about it some more?" she asked quietly.

He didn't say anything for a moment and she thought he wasn't going to. Disappointment trickled through her.

His fingers tightened on her. "Yeah."

She smiled, so many emotions clogging her throat. "Okay." She wished she'd been with him, been there to hold him.

"After something like that happens to you, you have to alter your view of yourself and who you are," he said. "Before, I was an ex-mercenary, a big brother, a berserker. It's hard when all that ends in a blink of an eye."

"You're still all those things," she insisted.

"I know. But I'm different, too. I had to rewrite my view of myself. Not better or worse, just different. Now I'm an ex-mercenary, a big brother, an ex-berserker, and head of the firing range and armory for the Enclave."

"You're a pretty amazing man, Manu Rahia."

He smiled. "How about you show me how amazing?"

"Again? I have twenty minutes until my shift starts—"

He shifted, rolling her beneath him. "Then you'd better be quick."

HIS BODY RELAXED and blood still humming, Manu stepped out into the sunshine. He felt happy. Even when his prosthetic foot caught on a rock and he had to catch himself, he smiled.

Kate was one step ahead of him, and damn, she looked good in her armor.

He loved that only he got to see under all her various types of armor. The physical and the emotional. She must have felt his gaze on her, because she glanced back at him. When her gaze met his, her cheeks went pink, and he grinned, knowing just what she was thinking about. She smiled back, and damn if he didn't feel like he'd won the damned lottery.

"I want to check out the mine site from last night," she said.

He nodded, and they walked quietly toward the patch of ground. In the distance, he saw the berserkers. They surrounded the small figure of Selena who was doing her thing to find the landmines. Tane was one step behind the woman, looking pissed off.

"So, Tane and Selena?" Kate said.

Manu grunted. "No idea what is going on there."

"Then you're blind."

He wasn't blind. He just wasn't sure he wanted his brother falling for an alien woman with strange, powerful abilities. But that was a concern for another time.

As they approached the crater, he felt the growing tension pumping off Kate. He gripped the nape of her neck reassuringly. He knew she was reliving every moment of the attack the night before. She'd checked in on Kendra, but the woman had been sleeping. He knew Kate was taking it hard.

Manu waited for his own memories to surface, but they were strangely silent.

The mine remnants had been removed. Kate skidded down the side of the hole, looking around the bottom of the crater.

"How are they digging these in here?" she said. "Even digging a small tunnel takes time."

"They must have some sort of tech that does it for them."

She carefully prodded the dirt around her feet with her boot. And a second later, some of the dirt fell inward, tumbling away like a small waterfall.

She'd uncovered a tunnel buried in the ground below.

Manu frowned. "Kate."

But she was already crouching by the hole and leaning her head into it to look around. He watched as she pulled a flashlight off her belt and flicked it on.

"It looks intact," she said. "It's big enough for a man to crawl through."

"It's too dangerous," he said.

"We need to stop them, Manu. I'm damn well going to make sure that no one else gets hurt."

"Fuck." He wasted no time skidding down into the crater, ignoring the ache in his leg. Then he touched his ear. "Enclave, we found a small, intact tunnel beneath the explosion site."

"Okay, Manu," Indy replied. "What's your plan?"

He looked at Kate. She nodded.

Manu sighed. "We'll follow it, as long as it's safe."

"Acknowledged. We'll likely lose signal with you, so be careful."

"Give us thirty minutes. If we're not back by then, send out the cavalry." He glanced across the field to his old squad.

"You got it, Manu. Stay safe."

"Sure thing, gorgeous."

When he looked up, Kate closed the comm line and raised a brow. "Gorgeous?"

He smiled, liking the edge to her voice. "Indy is like a sister to me."

"But she's not your sister. She's a beautiful, vibrant woman."

The edge had deepened, and he yanked Kate close. "And I happen to like tough, serious women with a hidden side of wild."

He leaned down and nipped her lips. She tried to pull away, but he held her close.

"You still feel me, Kate?"

"What?"

"Between your legs."

"Manu."

"Oh, my God, you guys." Indy's excited voice came across the comm line. "I don't know what you guys are talking about, but you know, I have a drone on you. Saw that kiss. You guys are *hot* together."

Kate groaned and touched her earpiece. "Heading into the tunnel now, Indy." She gave Manu a scorching look, then turned and dropped down into the tunnel.

Manu followed her. He would have preferred to be in

the lead, but he knew she'd fight him on it. Still, it was no hardship to crawl behind and watch her ass.

An ass he'd touched, kissed, and clenched in his hands. *Shit*. He didn't need a hard-on right now.

She aimed the light ahead and they crawled along the narrow tunnel. It was uncomfortable crawling on his knee, but he ignored it.

"Tunnel is still intact," she called back.

It was a tight fit. Not for Kate, but Manu's shoulders brushed the edges of the tunnel. It smelled like ripe earth, and the roots of grass and various plants dangled beside them.

Lucky he wasn't claustrophobic.

As they continued onward, the tunnel widened, and soon opened up enough that they could stand.

He moved up beside Kate, cradling his carbine.

"This part of the tunnel looks older," he said.

She flashed the light around, studying the walls. "You're right. This has been dug into rock, and it looks like it's been here a while. I think we're inside one of the neighboring coal mines."

He nodded, and they continued down the wider tunnel. He could imagine mine workers moving through here on their way to dig up more coal.

A dark, bulky shadow loomed ahead. He tensed, then quickly relaxed when he realized they were crates.

For a second, he thought it was abandoned gear from when the mine had been active. But as they got closer, his gut clenched. The crates were made of bone.

"Fuck," he muttered.

"Gizzida." Kate moved to the nearest one and nudged the lid aside.

The crate was filled with Gizzida landmines.

"Holy hell," Manu growled. "Look at all those damn things."

Kate cursed. "We have to stop them."

CHAPTER TWELVE

Kate's fury was incandescent. The aliens were attacking them right under their fucking noses. She barely stopped herself from kicking the crates of landmines.

"Let's keep looking around," Manu said, a frown on his face.

She looked at her watch. "We only have another fifteen minutes left before we need to check in."

"We'll be quick."

They continued down the tunnel, passing several shadowed side tunnels, with more crates of landmines stacked against the walls. So many. Too many. "Manu, we have to get back and report in."

He grunted, and she took that as agreement.

Frustration chewed on her. She wanted to take action. She wanted to *do* something. But she forced herself to turn around. The general and Niko needed to know what was going on.

They headed back the way they'd come. She didn't relish the thought of wiggling back through the small tunnel, but the quicker they got back, the quicker they could come up with a plan to deal with the raptors and their damn landmines.

A harsh, scraping sound caught her ear and she stilled.

Manu paused, his head cocked. He lifted his carbine. He'd heard it, too.

Shit, should she turn her flashlight off? She stared at a tunnel that speared off to their left. It was small and dark. She squinted, trying to see through the thick blackness.

Suddenly, a group of raptors burst out of the darkness.

Shit. Kate whipped her carbine up and fired.

Manu was firing too, laser fire lighting up the dark cavern, casting wild shadows on the walls. A raptor leaped at Kate and his big, scaly body slammed into her.

Dammit. They hit the ground and the alien's heavy weight knocked the wind out of her. Her carbine flew out of her hands. Fighting to draw a breath, she scrambled for the Gladius attached to her belt. She yanked the combat knife out and stabbed it into the raptor's side.

He grunted and she stabbed again, thanking her lucky stars that the exoskeleton built into her armor gave her extra strength. The raptor flopped on her, lifeless, and with a grunt, she heaved his weight off.

When she leaped to her feet, she took in the fight before her. Two raptors were attacking Manu, fighting hand to hand.

He was ducking and weaving, and getting in several

good blows. She watched one raptor's head snap back from Manu's punch.

The other rushed forward with a guttural grunt, and Manu went down on one knee, slamming a fist into the gut of the second raptor. The raptor stumbled back into the first one, and they both staggered.

Kate spotted the light on her carbine on the ground, snatched her weapon up and took aim. A few well-placed shots, and both raptors slumped to the floor.

"Let's go," she called out.

Manu jumped up.

Suddenly, she heard a strange clicking sound. They spun, pressed close together, both staring down their scopes.

A nightmare appeared at the end of the tunnel. A huge, spider-like creature with six legs and a glowing red belly. The creature almost filled the entire tunnel.

A creeper.

She'd heard all about these damn creatures. They had huge, sucking mouths that could swallow a human whole. They then kept their victim in their bellies, where they injected them with alien DNA and turned them into raptors.

She started firing. Manu reached over his shoulder and pulled off a large shotgun. He lifted the weapon as the creeper rushed forward. It raised its two front legs. One leg crashed down close to Kate, knocking the carbine out of her hands. The weapon skidded across the dirt-packed floor, and when the creeper reared again, its leg smashed down, destroying her weapon with a crunch of metal. The flashlight was still functioning, illuminating the creeper in a beam of white light.

Wicked-sharp legs reared again.

"Kate! Move."

She rolled out of the way. The boom of a shotgun reverberated off the walls and the creeper screeched, pulling back. One of its legs was dangling at an odd angle.

Kate rolled to her feet and pulled the elite carbine Manu had given her off her shoulder. Despite being wounded, the creeper wasn't done, and it skittered in again. Kate moved closer to Manu and they fired together. The whine of her carbine mingled with the boom of the shotgun.

The creeper's belly exploded and red-orange goo splattered all over them. The creeper collapsed and, grimacing, Kate lifted her arm, swiping it across her face. *Ugh.*

Threat eradicated, she looked up at Manu, and he grinned at her. He had a streak of red gunk on his cheek. She smiled back.

Another skittering sound. Her gut hardened.

"Fuck," Manu muttered.

It was lighter than the sound of the creeper, but she doubted it meant things were better.

She turned, aiming her light toward the shadowed end of the tunnel. Dozens of active landmines skittered toward them on tiny legs.

Hell. She started firing again. Manu joined in, muttering more curses. But there were hundreds of the damn things.

The laser cartridge on her carbine blinked out. *Dammit*. She quickly switched it to projectile mode, unloading thermo bullets into the mines.

Very quickly, Kate and Manu were surrounded. They had nowhere to go. *Shit*.

"Drop your weapons." The English words were said in a deep, guttural voice.

Her head jerked up. *Double shit*. Several raptors were striding toward them, weapons aimed. She quickly glanced at Manu and saw that his face had gone hard.

The lead raptor had a red-leather bandolier over his scaled chest, and she guessed that denoted some sort of rank. He nodded at one of his raptors, and the alien stepped forward, the bombs moving to clear room for him. He aimed his poison-filled weapon at Kate's head, red eyes burning into hers.

Manu lowered his shotgun and, chest tight, Kate did the same. She let her modified carbine drop to the ground.

More bombs danced out of the way as another raptor strode forward. Kate opened her mouth to speak, but the raptor moved, landing a vicious blow to Manu's head.

It was so sudden.

"Hey!" she cried out.

Manu staggered sideways and hit the ground hard. He was out cold. She moved to help him, but sharp claws gripped the back of her neck, stopping her.

The raptor who'd hit Manu leaned down, grabbed the back of his armor, and started dragging him down the tunnel.

Anger burned through Kate, hot and molten. She

lifted her head to blast the raptors, but a large, scaled fist was coming right at her head.

Pain exploded and blackness swallowed her.

MANU CAME to with his head throbbing. Wincing, he took stock. He was sitting slumped against a hard wall. Low, red lighting glowed all around him.

Something warm brushed his cheek.

"Thank God."

He opened his eyes to see Kate watching him, stroking his cheek.

When his vision came fully into focus, he could see her cheek was swollen and smudged with dried blood. Fury exploded inside him. Whoever had hit her would pay.

Focus, Rahia. He realized they were sitting in a large cavern, and he heard raptors talking close by. A lot of raptors. He couldn't damn well take them all down.

Suddenly, he realized that his weapons were gone. Carbine gone. Shotgun gone. Knife gone.

"You okay?" he murmured.

She nodded. "I've been more worried about you. Damn raptor clobbered you really hard."

"I have a pretty hard head."

A faint smile crossed her face, and his gaze dropped to her lips. Damn, even in the worst of circumstances, looking at her mouth still made him think about sex.

Manu looked over her shoulder. A group of raptors

sat around a small fire, eating. He watched one lift a leg of meat and tear into it with sharp teeth.

Scanning their surroundings, he saw they were in some sort of large, open area underground. The ceiling was rocky, but the walls were covered in some sort of concrete. Hulking mining equipment was parked off to one side, glowing dully in the red lights the aliens had set up to illuminate the tunnels.

"We need to get out of here," he said.

She nodded, then she pointed.

That's when he saw an entire wall full of crates loaded with landmines. Except these bombs were far bigger than the ones they'd been defusing so far. *Fucking hell.*

"Small ones were a test," he mused.

She nodded. "They're planning to attack the Enclave."

"Options?"

Her luscious mouth moved into a flat line. "Limited."

He looked again at the group of raptors and saw that the only way out of the room was on the other side of them. Kate was right. They only had shitty options. He looked back at her bruised face.

"We need to set some of the bombs off."

Her eyes went wide. "What?"

"Cause a mess, and in the chaos, we can escape."

"Shit." She scraped a hand through her tangled hair. He could see that she was thinking. "Shit."

He nodded. "I know it's not the greatest plan."

"It's all we have." She straightened her shoulders. "We'll make it work." Then she leaned over and kissed him. "Just don't get yourself killed. That would really piss me off."

"I really don't want to piss you off." He smiled. "Think I must be growing on you."

She smiled. "Maybe."

"Let's do it."

The raptors weren't paying them any attention. Together, they both moved into a crouch and snuck slowly along the wall. They reached the first box of mines, and Manu stuck his hand in, and pulled one out. He pried open the side of the bomb and activated it. Little legs unfurled, wiggling.

He handed it to her and grabbed another one.

"Ready?" he asked.

She pulled in a deep breath, lifting her bomb. She nodded.

"Three, two, one." They both tossed the bombs toward the raptors.

Clunk. Clunk.

Out of the corner of his eye, Manu saw one raptor leap to his feet. Rasping shouts echoed through the cavern. Then the first bomb exploded.

Screams and grunts filled the air and Manu grabbed Kate's arm.

"Go, go!" he urged her.

They jumped up and sprinted, sticking close to the wall. Suddenly, poison splattered the rock wall just behind them. Clearly, some raptors had survived the blasts.

A raptor jumped in front of them. Manu aimed a kick into the alien. He grabbed the raptor's scaly arms, swinging him around. After a quick scuffle, Manu managed to yank the alien's weapon off him. He spun it around and fired at close range.

The raptor fell backward, but there were more shouts of alarm. Another group of raptors was rushing toward them.

He took a second to glance over at Kate. She was wrestling with another raptor. They spun in an unwieldy circle, and a second later, she and her opponent slammed into a stack of landmine crates.

"Kate!" Manu shouted.

The crates tumbled, and landmines rolled out like bowling balls. Kate tried to stay on her feet, but slipped on the bombs. The raptor fell over with a shout.

Manu saw some of the bombs blink on, activating.

No. He sprinted toward her, jumping and dodging the rolling balls. He imagined he was back on the rugby field. She was toppling over when he reached her. He scooped her up, kicked the raptor in the face, and leaped over the last of the bombs.

Then he aimed toward the mining equipment, lungs burning as he ran as fast as he could.

The gear was old and rusted, but it was built of solid steel. He hoped to hell it would hold against multiple explosions.

He jumped, and they flew into the space between the equipment and the wall.

They landed hard, both of them grunting. A huge explosion ripped through the cavern behind them.

Manu rolled on top of Kate to shield her. Dirt rained down on them, and debris made loud pinging sounds, bouncing off the metal machines. More explosions followed, shaking the ground.

He felt something hit his prosthetic leg. The pain receptors flared and he jerked. Then everything went quiet.

"Okay?" Kate whispered.

"Yeah. Something hit my prosthetic leg, but I'm fine. Let's move while we can."

He rolled off her and they jumped up. He grabbed her hand, and they slid out from behind the equipment.

But luck wasn't on their side.

Manu's gut went rock solid. Several battered, blood-covered raptors stood with weapons aimed at them. The lead raptor, his bandolier torn and hanging off him, was among them, his eyes burning with fury.

Manu tightened his grip on Kate. *Fuck.*

CHAPTER THIRTEEN

K ate groaned and rolled over. God, her body hurt. Even her teeth hurt.

She lifted her head and peered blearily around the space. Close by, she could hear the grunts of raptors talking.

Dammit. Where was Manu? She turned her head and her chest went tight.

He was hanging from chains strung up over the mining equipment. His arms were wrenched above his head and his chin was resting on his chest. His armor was gone, and his shirt was torn and bloody.

Was he alive? Terror filled her. She'd never felt this desperate, pained emotion before. She got up on her knees and finally acknowledged the true depth of her feelings for this man. It had happened fast, was too soon, but it was real.

Quietly, she crawled over to him, trying not to attract

any attention. They'd been gone too long now, so she was sure the squads would be on their way.

If the squads could find their way through the maze of mining tunnels.

She touched one of Manu's legs. "Manu?"

She saw that his prosthetic leg was damaged. His trousers were torn, exposing the damaged limb. Probably from the blasts earlier. She also saw something else.

Scales had appeared on his leg, the same as had happened with Kendra. *What the hell?*

Suddenly, Manu's body jerked, and relief flooded her. He was alive. Her heart shot into her throat as she rose. She reached up and cupped his jaw.

"Manu?"

"Kate." His voice was dry and croaky.

"You okay?"

"Sure." He lifted his head, looking around. He tested his restraints. "Can't get free."

Now, Kate scanned the cavern. They needed a way to get out of here. But all she could see were more crates of those damn landmines. No other weapons in sight.

"Kate."

She turned her gaze to meet his. "I'm going to—"

"Get out of here."

Her eyes widened. "And leave you here?" Her words were a furious whisper.

"Yes."

Ignoring him, she spotted an empty crate. She nudged it over in front of him.

"Get out and warn the Enclave," he continued.

"They'd already know something went wrong. We've been gone way longer than thirty minutes."

"I don't want my brothers walking into this clusterfuck."

"We are getting out of here," she said sternly. She stood up on the crate and checked the chains. They were face to face.

"I don't want you here, either. Get out, Kate."

She glanced into velvet-brown eyes, warmth in her chest. "Not. Leaving. You." She fiddled with the chains.

He let out a sigh. "Fine. There's a knife in my boot."

Of course there was. Badass Manu Rahia wouldn't go anywhere without a backup weapon. She crouched down, found the hidden slot in the side of his boot, and yanked the knife out.

When she stood, she took a second to press her lips to his. "For a second, I thought you were dead."

His eyes flashed. "Kate."

"Manu, I—" She tried to put some words to her emotions, but damn, she wasn't good at this.

He smiled. "I know."

She nodded. Now wasn't the time to talk, but hopefully they'd get the chance later. She lifted the knife and tried to pry open the lock on the chains.

A guttural laugh sounded behind her and she quickly spun.

Several raptors fanned out, watching them. *Dammit*. Despair washed over her.

When she looked back, she saw Manu's face was hard.

The lead raptor, bandolier now repaired, stepped

forward. "I want to know the easiest way to get my weapons into your base."

Kate straightened. "Screw you."

He stepped closer and with her standing on the crate, they were almost face-to-face. "Humans are so stubborn."

She lifted her chin. "Yep."

His hand flashed out and he punched her in the gut. Pain exploded and she doubled over.

Behind her, she heard Manu's chains rattle.

"Don't fucking touch her," Manu ground out.

Kate breathed through the pain. "Just kill us. There's no way we'll give up our people."

The raptor shot her an ugly smile. "We have ways to make people talk."

She choked out a laugh. "It'll never happen."

The raptor gripped the front of her shirt, jerking her to her toes. "Let's see how much *he* can take."

She glared. "He'll never break. He's stronger than all of us."

An ugly smile unfurled on the raptor's face. She stiffened, her stomach turning over.

"Let's see how much he can take of watching what we do to you before he breaks."

Manu made a choked, growling sound, and Kate felt ice slide through her veins.

PANIC WAS an ugly burn in Manu's gut.

He watched a raptor drag a chair over in front of him.

It was beaten up and looked like it was left over from when the mine had been in operation.

Another raptor yanked Kate by the hair and dragged her to the chair. He shoved her into it. She was silent, defiance wafting off her, as they tied her to the chair.

So tough, his woman. So perfect.

"Come on, then," she ground out. "Hit me."

"Kate," Manu warned.

Her blue eyes were blazing. "I can take it. Don't give them anything."

Manu gritted his teeth.

The head raptor talked to another, and a second later, a third raptor walked closer. He was carrying a small black box.

He walked up to Kate, and her gaze fell on the box.

The head raptor leaned over and opened the lid.

Manu craned his neck, and saw a small silver device nestled in the center of the box. It looked long and skinny, but he was too far away to see it clearly.

"Can you get a move on?" Kate said, voice bored.

The raptor lifted the device. "We call this a *baraa*."

Kate didn't say anything, but she swallowed. The raptor held out his scaly palm and Manu saw the thing wiggle.

"It will enter your body through your nose," the raptor said.

Fuck. Manu tested the chains again, but they were too strong.

"It will burrow its way to your brain and into your brain tissue."

Kate lifted her chin another inch.

"Then you'll be very willing to share what you know. This little thing will destroy areas in your brain that regulate your self-control."

She thrashed against her chair, and Manu wanted to be sick. Then, he wanted to slam the fucking raptor's head into the wall.

The raptor leaned down, bringing the small creature closer to Kate's face. He put it on her cheek and it wiggled. She thrashed again.

"Hold her," the lead raptor ordered.

Two raptor soldiers stepped up, pinning her down to the chair.

"Leave her alone," Manu barked.

The leader looked his way. "You'll share all the entrances to your base? And security details?"

"Manu, no!" Kate shouted.

God, so many innocent people were in the Enclave—women, children, injured survivors. His gaze fell on Kate. The woman who matched him step for step. The woman he wanted for his own.

He roared his frustration, rattling his chains.

The raptor turned back to Kate and watched his little device wiggle into Kate's nose.

"I'm afraid after the *baraa* is finished, it is impossible to extract," the leader added.

She jerked, her eyes wide.

"It will liquefy your brain."

Fuck, no. Manu felt a sense of fury-fueled power wash through him. No way was he going to let his woman be killed right before his eyes.

Using his strength, he lifted his legs up to his chest.

The raptor nearby tensed, but Manu kicked out, knocking him into another raptor.

Fast, Manu curled and lifted his legs all the way up, smashing his prosthetic against the chains above his head.

Nothing happened. He lifted his left leg again, using all his strength to bang the high-tech titanium alloy against the chains.

One chain broke, and his body dropped. One of his hands was free.

The lead raptor shouted something, and Manu guessed it was orders to stop him. *Not today, asshole.*

A raptor rushed him and Manu kicked out again. The raptor staggered. Manu lifted his leg once more and bashed it into the other chain.

It broke open and he dropped to the ground in a crouch. *Free.*

Raptors rushed at him, but his fury was white-hot, flooding him with adrenaline. He was going to save his fucking woman.

Enraged, he snatched up one of the chains and swung out with it. A raptor went down under the vicious swing. Manu punched and kicked. He ducked and dodged blows. His prosthetic was badly damaged, and his balance was off, but he stayed on his feet and kept fighting.

He landed a punch into the chest of another raptor. The alien dropped his weapon, and quickly, Manu snatched it up.

He spun, opening fire. Poison sprayed everywhere.

He watched the lead raptor duck out of the way,

some of his men covering him. Manu kept firing, charging forward to reach Kate.

He reached her chair and, with the weapon still up, he used his boot to slam down through the ropes binding her.

She bounded up and scooped another discarded weapon off the floor.

Together, they started firing and walking backward.

"Tunnel," he yelled.

She nodded. They kept up a steady spray of poison, keeping the raptors from getting close.

Then they turned and ran for the tunnel.

CHAPTER FOURTEEN

Adrenaline charged through Kate's veins as they powered through the darkened tunnels. Red lights up near the roof still provided some illumination, but they were spaced farther apart, leaving big patches of darkness.

Her body was throbbing with pain, but then she felt a sharp sting in her nose. Shit, she'd forgotten about the *baraa*.

She stumbled to a stop. "Manu."

He pulled up. "We have to—"

"Get it out." She pinched her nose. "Get this damn thing out of me."

He cursed and tilted her face up. "I can see the end of it." He brought his fingers up near her nostril and pinched them together.

He must have been able to grab the end of it, because she felt it wriggle. *Ugh*. Her stomach rolled. The damn thing was almost fully inside her nose.

Panic flared and bile rose in her throat. "Get it out."

With a nod, he started to pull. The thing fought back. The sting turned to burning pain, and tears poured down her cheeks. *Oh, God. Don't be sick, Kate.*

Manu hesitated.

"Do it," she rasped. "I want it out." Her skin was crawling, and she was horribly aware that the raptors could find them at any second.

Manu resumed tugging. Kate bit her lip. It felt like there was a burning-hot poker up her nose. She tasted blood.

And suddenly, with one, final spike of pain, Manu yanked the thing free. It was wriggling around wildly, and he dropped it on the dirt floor. With one big stomp of his boot, it was gone.

Kate felt a trickle of blood from her nose and swiped at it with her knuckle.

"Babe." Manu cupped her jaw.

"I'm okay." She hugged him, hard. She needed his strength. "Thank you."

"We have to keep moving." His hand tangled in her hair. "They'll be looking for us."

She nodded.

They kept moving, silent and wary, their weapons held at the ready. Kate noticed Manu's uneven gait and realized he was limping badly. But his face was set and resolute, so she didn't bring it up.

"Any idea where we are?" she asked.

"No clue."

They kept moving, hoping against hope that they were increasing the distance between them and the raptors, with only the ominous red lighting illuminating their way. She searched for any tunnel that looked familiar, but everything freaking looked the same. They traveled down one dark tunnel, only to reach an area where dirt and rock filled the passage. The tunnel was partially collapsed.

"Dammit." Manu gripped her arm and yanked her back the way they'd come.

They turned another corner.

"The odds of finding the tunnel we used to get here are slim," she said. "We need to just find a way to the surface. Any way."

He nodded.

She noticed his limp was getting worse. "You okay? Looks like your prosthetic is damaged."

"It'll hold up," he said grimly. "Keep going."

But their pace was getting slower and slower. Kate was pretty sure they were headed for another fight about her leaving him behind.

She wasn't leaving him. *Ever*.

They were walking down another dark tunnel, when an eerie sound echoed through the labyrinth behind them, causing them to both jerk to a halt. They glanced back, staring into the darkness.

Yips of excited animals resonated down the tunnel, followed by a long, drawn-out howl that made the hairs on the back of her neck rise.

"Fuck." Manu looked at his boots, his hands clenching on the raptor weapon. "They've set canids on us."

She knew the alien hunting dogs were vicious. "Let's keep moving."

Glad for her weapon, even though she hated the scaly feel of it, she hefted it higher as they trudged down the tunnel. Surely it was time for them to catch a break.

But then something appeared out of the gloom, sending her hope spiraling downward.

A rock wall.

It was a dead end.

"Dammit." Apparently, Lady Luck had decided to toy with them today. Kate turned, the sounds of the canids getting louder.

"We'll have to make a stand here," Manu said.

They were stuck in a dead end with no cover, and only two alien weapons between them. Her throat burned.

"Kate." He pulled her close.

Her fingers tightened on his arms. "I know," she whispered.

They shared a moment of silence, the air between them charged. It was really unfair that she'd met a man who was perfect for her—who she didn't scare or intimidate, who made her light up and melt, who looked at her like she was the most gorgeous thing he'd ever seen—only for them to die in this horrible, dark, dusty place.

"I have some grenades," he said.

Her eyebrows rose. "The raptors didn't take them?"

His teeth were white in the darkness. "They were hidden in my first aid kit. I made them look like rolls of bandages."

She managed a smile. "Sneaky."

He leaned heavily against the wall as he fished out the grenades. "I have a cedar oil one the canids won't like, and a new cineole one that the tech team are still testing. Plus a couple of regular frag grenades."

As he talked, she looked down at those ugly scales covering his prosthetic. It looked like they were chewing through the high-tech metal.

God, if his prosthetic broke before they got out of here, he wouldn't be able to walk. Without her armor, she wouldn't be able to carry him.

"Set up two of these near the entrance," he said.

She nodded, taking the grenades, and moved down the tunnel. She crouched low, placing them carefully.

Back by his side, they stood, shoulder to shoulder, and both lifted their weapons.

A deep growl rumbled through the darkness.

Her nerves stretched taut. The alien dog was close. She clutched her weapon, keeping her hands steady.

Then the first canid slunk out of the darkness.

MANU WATCHED as the alien hunting dog crept forward.

Ugly bastard. The canine-like alien had thick, tough skin, sharp spikes along its back, and drool dripping off the fangs in its jaws.

The first grenade exploded with an earsplitting *bang*, blowing the canid apart.

But before they could celebrate, more canids rushed into the tunnel. The second grenade—the cedar oil one—went off. Pained yelps reverberated off the walls.

Manu started firing, a grim smile on his face. Kate opened fire at the same time. He and Kate might be backed into a corner, but they wouldn't go down easily.

Poison splattered the walls and floor, sizzling, and canids howled in pain and anger.

Behind the dogs, the big, hulking shapes of raptors formed out of the gloom.

Poison sprayed nearby, and Manu dodged closer to Kate. She barely flinched, still returning fire. More poison hit the ground, and he felt some hit his prosthetic.

A second later, his leg went out from under him.

He dropped to his knees. Fuck, his prosthetic was ruined.

Suddenly, bone projectiles hit the wall above his head. *Thump. Thump. Thump.*

"Kate, sniper!"

She ducked down, still firing.

"Kate." He pulled his last grenade—the experimental cineole one—off his belt. "I'll create a diversion and you get out."

She eyed the grenade. "What?"

"Get out."

She shook her head. "No."

"I love you. I want you out and safe."

Her eyes widened. "Not leaving, Rahia." She turned away to spray more fire at the raptors. "I'm pretty sure I'm in love with you, too."

She sounded pissed. Sweet pain and savage satisfaction filled him. "Babe."

More bone projectiles whizzed through the air and they ducked.

"You light me up," she said angrily. "Before you, I was existing, not living. You gave me color, life. You made me *feel*."

"Kate." She was slicing him up inside.

"You gave me a reason to fight, Manu. A reason to survive, and to damn well live."

She fired again, and then he followed with several shots of his own.

"We're getting out of here," she snapped. "Got it?"

He eyed the tunnel, and the wave of raptors approaching. Kate cursed, and Manu felt like a rock had settled in his gut.

"We both get out," she said, "or we both go down fighting."

God, she was one hell of a woman. "I love you, babe."

"And I love you right back, you stubborn, alpha male."

They kept firing, the tunnel ripe with the smell of burning poison and flesh. A moment later, Manu's alien weapon clicked on empty. *Dammit*. He dropped it.

Kate edged closer to him, still firing. Fuck, he hated feeling helpless. The last time he'd felt like this was when he'd lost his leg. When he'd been screaming in agony and unable to move.

The raptors were trying to take the damn planet. They'd taken his leg, and now they were trying to take away the one woman who meant everything to him.

Suddenly, Kate jerked back. He looked up and the

bottom dropped out of his stomach at the sight of a bone projectile lodged in her shoulder.

"Kate!"

Another volley of projectiles. Pain sliced into his gut. Grimly, he saw a bone bolt had speared through his stomach.

He reached down and yanked it out. He grimaced and tried to ignore the agony.

Kate's body jerked to the side, and he saw she'd been hit again. She fell down on the dirt floor with a cry.

He reached out to her, helplessness choking him. *Fuck, no.* It wasn't going to end like this.

KATE TRIED to block out the pain of the projectiles buried in her shoulder and side. She could feel blood soaking her shirt and knew it was bad.

She also felt any remaining energy seeping out of her. She dragged herself over to Manu and grabbed his hand.

She sensed the last of the raptors getting closer, but she ignored them, too.

All she could see was Manu. His face was covered in blood and grime, but he smiled at her.

"You are my perfect woman."

She laughed. "I love you, too, Manu."

He held up one more grenade.

"Thought you were out."

"Old habit. Always save one. Ready to take the last of these suckers down?"

"Hell, yeah."

Manu lobbed the grenade, and they both ducked down. It exploded with a deafening bang, which was followed by raptor grunts and groans. A haze filled the small tunnel and smelled like eucalyptus.

The raptors' cries increased. She raised her head and saw several aliens clutching their heads, blood pouring from their noses, eyes, and mouths. *Holy hell.*

But a fresh wave of raptors leaped over the injured. One charged toward them out of the haze. He grabbed Kate and dragged her up off the ground. She kicked him, sending him stumbling into the rock wall. Kate gripped the bone projectile stuck in her shoulder and yanked it out. The pain was horrible, making her eyes water. But she gritted her teeth and breathed through it. When the raptor looked up with a growl, she stabbed the projectile through his eye.

He let out a scream. He released her and dropped his weapon.

Excellent. As she dropped back to her knees, Manu snatched up the weapon. He took aim and fired at the other raptors.

After a few moments, no more aliens emerged from the dissipating smoke. Her breath hitched. Had they really beaten them all?

Unable to hold herself upright any longer, she collapsed to the ground.

"Shit," Manu bit out, collapsing down beside her. He pulled her closer and slumped against the wall.

"What?" She rested her head on his chest.

"I think I'm going to pass out."

She gripped his hand. "You can't. I can't carry you."

He cursed again. "Fuck. That won't stop you from trying, though, will it?"

This time, she shot him a grin.

She'd drag him out of here like a caveman, if she had to. But then, she heard a shout in the distance, the sound echoing down the tunnel. Her heart dropped. It was in the raptor language.

More raptors were incoming, and she knew Manu couldn't withstand another round. She squeezed his hand, and they sat there in silence.

When the first raptor appeared at the entrance to the tunnel, a numbing calm slipped over Kate. She was with Manu and that was what mattered to her. More raptors appeared, all cradling their weapons.

This was it.

Kate took a deep breath.

Suddenly, the ground beneath them started to vibrate. Dirt trickled down from the roof. The raptors looked upward, confused.

"What the hell?" Kate muttered.

With a violent explosion of rock, the wall to their left exploded outward. Kate gasped as the metallic tip of a large drill burst through the rock. A huge piece of mining equipment rattled into the tunnel, crashing into the raptors.

She blinked, unable to believe her eyes. Hemi and Tane were behind the controls.

"Woo-hoo!" Hemi called out.

They continued down the tunnel, crashing through more raptors. From the newly bored hole behind the drill, the berserkers rushed out—Levi, Ash, Dom, and Griff. Green laser fire lit up the tunnel.

It didn't take long for them to mow down the remaining raptors.

"Fuck." Griff raced toward Manu and Kate. He dropped down beside them and then yanked something off his belt. He pressed some wadded gauze to Kate's shoulder, putting pressure on her wound.

Dom appeared and started work on Manu.

"How you doing there, Captain?" Griff asked.

"It's Kate." She stared at his hard, but handsome, face.

"How are you doing, Kate?"

"I've had better days."

Now she got a faint smile. "We'll be back at the Enclave before you know it."

"How'd you find us?"

"We'd been searching the tunnels for a while when we heard the commotion. Got one of the geek squad's mini-drones operational and headed this way."

"What a damn mess," came a deep, gravelly voice.

Kate looked up. Marcus Steele and the rest of Hell Squad were also coming out of the newly-drilled tunnel.

Hell Squad's sniper, Shaw, frowned, his sniper rifle pressed up to his shoulder. "Well, hell. How come nobody left us any raptors to kill?"

Griff patted Kate's arm, drawing her attention back to him. His face was hard and worried. "You'll be in the infirmary in the blink of an eye."

"Not a fan of doctors, so you aren't making me feel

any better." She swallowed. "How's Manu?" Griff was blocking her view.

"That tough guy will be fine."

But she saw Griff glance up at Tane, who was standing close by. Squad Three's leader didn't look happy. His face was blank, his mouth tight.

Then Dom's near-accent-less voice cut through the air. "Manu? Hey, stay with us, my man."

"Manu." Kate tried to sit up.

Griff planted a hand on her chest and held her down. "Stay still, Kate. We need to stop your bleeding."

"Manu—"

"He's passed out, but he's breathing."

"Shit, what's wrong with his leg?" Hemi bit out.

Kate managed to shove Griff aside and get a look at Manu.

She gasped. The alien scales had multiplied and were covering most of what was left of his prosthetic. They had just started to crawl up the skin of his thigh.

"Let's get them to the infirmary," Tane ordered. "Now!"

CHAPTER FIFTEEN

Griff

Griff ducked through the reinforced doorway, pushing the iono-stretcher into the Enclave. *Thank fuck.* He hated being out in the open with injured people.

His squad mates followed him in, all of them covered in dirt, sweat, and grime. Hell Squad had stayed behind to clean out the mine tunnels of any remaining aliens. They had orders to seal up the neighboring mine in any way possible. Griff was certain that would involve explosives. He suspected Hemi would have liked to help make that mess, but the guy was clearly worried about his brother.

Griff leaned over the stretcher, his gaze falling on Manu and Kate. She'd refused to get on her own stretcher. Manu was unconscious, and Kate was wrapped around him. She'd been whispering nonstop to him the entire trip back.

It was strange to see tough, no-nonsense Captain Kate Scott clearly head over heels for the oldest Rahia brother. He'd pegged her as cool, but seeing her with Manu made it clear she wasn't.

Even though Manu was unconscious, the man knew his woman was with him. He had one strong arm wrapped around her, and he'd held tight to her the entire trip back.

They fit. Even Griff, who'd had his faith in women and relationships shattered into jagged pieces long ago, could see these two fit.

Kate hadn't left Manu. Griff glanced at Manu's mangled leg. He would have asked her to go and find a way out. Griff knew his friend well, and Manu would've wanted Kate out of there.

But she'd stayed. She'd fought at his side.

Unlike Griff's faithless ex-fiancée.

He shook his head. Now wasn't the time to think of Amelia.

"You're going to be fine, Manu," Kate murmured. "We're back at the Enclave."

Griff's fingers tightened on the stretcher.

"You brought color into my life." She pressed into Manu's side. "You brought me to life. I'm not letting you go."

Shit. Griff felt the hard shell around his heart crack a little.

Ahead, he heard running footsteps. Doc Emerson and her team appeared. Right behind them was another woman running fast on long legs, her dark ponytail flying out behind her. Indy.

Griff's gut clenched. He always felt that sensation whenever he saw her. He couldn't even remember when it started.

He'd grown up with Indy Bennett. Their families had been close friends and once, her brother Gareth had been his best friend. His brother.

For so many years, Indy had been Gareth's kid sister. At first, cute, then annoying and loud-mouthed. Then she'd reached her teens.

She'd always been fucking gorgeous, but at about sixteen, she'd started flirting and throwing herself at Griff. *Hell.* He'd held her off pretty successfully until she was eighteen. He'd been home on leave from the Police Academy with Gareth.

At a party, she'd cornered him and kissed the hell out of him. His fingers tightened. Damn, he'd wanted her.

But she'd been too young and wild, and more importantly, she'd been his best friend's little sister. Besides, he'd been focused on his career, passing the Academy, and working hard on his dream to be a cop like his dad.

To get Indy to back off, he'd been harsh with her. He'd hurt her.

His ruthless words about her being like a little sister to him, and that he'd never see her as a desirable woman had stopped the seduction attempts. Then she'd started avoiding him like the plague.

She'd also gone even wilder. She'd always been spirited, but over the next few years, the few times he'd seen her, he learned she'd gotten ink, been partying hard, and had a parade of biker and musician boyfriends.

A muscle ticked in his jaw. But he'd never stopped thinking about her. Hell, even when he'd been engaged to Amelia, he'd still had less-than-pure thoughts about Indy Bennett.

When he'd been incarcerated, she'd been one of the few people to come to see him in prison. He'd refused to see her.

His chest tightened. After the alien invasion and his escape from the supermax prison, he'd mourned his family, and he'd mourned Indy, too. He'd wake in the night, thinking about her.

Then he'd arrived at Blue Mountain Base and seen her among the survivors. Alive and more gorgeous than ever.

Indy had always been the color in his life.

"How are they?" She looked anxiously at the stretcher, worry etched on her face.

"They took down a buttload of raptors. They're battered, but tough as hell, both of them."

She glanced at him and nodded. Then her gaze moved past him to the rest of the squad. His fellow berserkers got a smile.

"Hey, babe." Hemi slapped her ass as he walked past.

"Neanderthal," she called out, no heat in the word. "Everyone in one piece? Nothing broken or bleeding?"

She didn't look at Griff. Once again, she was ignoring him.

Indy breathed life into a room, and he was sick of her pretending he didn't exist.

"You plan to kiss my boo-boos better?" Levi asked with a wink.

She smacked the tattooed man in the shoulder. "Chrissy would hit me in the head with her wrench, big guy. Then she'd come after you."

As the others headed down the corridor, Indy moved to follow them. Griff saw the tight lines bracketing her mouth. She was still worried. He gripped her arm, his hand wrapping around the bright rose tattoos on her skin.

"Manu and Kate will be all right," he said.

She nodded. "It's hard listening to the fighting over the comms, and not knowing if you guys will come back in one piece."

No way he'd be able to sit behind a desk and listen to the fighting. He'd always been a guy who preferred action, a man who believed in the law, and did whatever he had to do to protect it. He'd always thought right beat wrong, good beat evil. But life had taught him that wasn't always the case with a big fucking betrayal he'd never seen coming, followed by the damn alien invasion.

Without thinking, he tugged Indy in for a hug. She went still, then stiffened, and tried to pull back.

But Griff didn't want any distance between them and held her in place. She was a long, curvy handful, and smelled like she had years ago—of coconut.

"Let me go," she said.

"You're always avoiding me."

"No, I'm not. I see you every day."

"You look through me. You only look at me when you're busting my balls."

She glared at him. "Your balls are safe from me, Griff."

Some indefinable mix of emotion roared through him at her words, and he backed her into the wall.

Her gray eyes narrowed on his face. "Back off."

"I think it's time we talk about us."

"Us?" Her dark brows rose. "There is no us."

"Let's talk about why you've been avoiding me for years."

"Ah, you were in jail, Griff."

"Before that," he growled. He wanted no reminder of the years he'd spent in that hellhole.

"We grew up. You became a cop and left."

"Indy—"

"I'm not doing this." She shoved at him.

He grabbed her wrists, but she yanked one free and, quick as a snake, she slammed her open palm into his nose.

"Goddammit." He staggered back, checking she hadn't broken his nose.

"You taught me that self-defense move, remember? So I could deal with pushy guys who wouldn't take no for an answer."

"I'm not going to hurt you. I just want to talk." He glared at her.

"We have nothing to talk about."

"We are going to talk, Indy."

With a glare hot enough to melt his skin, she stomped off down the corridor.

Griff stayed where he was, watching the sway of her ass under her tight jeans. She was fighting him, but he'd been a cop a long time. He was good at reading people. He'd seen the flare of panic in her eyes when he'd told her they'd talk.

He thought of Kate's words to Manu. That he'd brought color to her life.

Griff had been ignoring the shades of gray around him for a very long time. Life had ground him down, but now he was finally ready to risk it all to get some color back into his world.

To get Indy back into his world.

KATE WOKE to a steady beeping sound and the smell of antiseptic. And thankfully, no pain.

She rolled over, looked at the ceiling and blinked. She was in the infirmary. She touched her shoulder and felt smooth skin, no sign of her wounds. No doubt she had a shot of nanomeds to thank for that.

She turned her head, and her gaze fell on Manu lying in the bed beside hers.

Her chest tightened and she sat up. His eyes were closed and he was lying so damn still.

She reached up and pulled a small sticky monitoring pad off her chest, then she swung her legs over the side of the bed. She was wearing a stupid hospital nightgown and was naked beneath it.

Carefully, she pressed her feet to the floor and waited. There was no dizziness. She crossed the few meters to Manu's bed and crawled in with him.

Curling around his body, she pressed her nose to his

throat and breathed him in. He was so still, but his skin was warm, and when she pressed her palm to his bare chest, she felt the steady thump of his heart.

She looked down and saw that the blanket on his lower left side lay flat. Her heart lodged in her throat. His prosthetic leg was gone and if she wasn't mistaken, some more of his thigh had been amputated. She stroked his chest. Once again, he had to face the hardship of rehab. She hugged him tighter. This time, she was going to be by his side every minute. She'd go out there herself and find him a new prosthetic, if she had to.

"A-hem."

Kate lifted her head and saw Emerson standing at the end of the bed, looking equal parts annoyed and amused.

"We frown on sharing beds in this infirmary," the doctor said.

Kate didn't move. "You'll have to drag me out."

Emerson just shook her head.

"She's not going anywhere," Manu rumbled.

Kate quickly looked back at him. "Manu." She touched his face, stroking his stubbled cheek. "How are you feeling?"

"Whenever I wake up with you, I feel pretty damn good."

God, he melted her. She pressed her lips to his.

When she pulled back, Emerson was grinning at them. "Well, you two went through the wringer, but you both have a clean bill of health now."

Kate clutched the sheet. "And Manu's leg?"

"I'm sorry." There was sympathy in Emerson's voice.

"Your prosthetic was completely destroyed and I was forced to amputate some more of your thigh."

Kate swallowed, and beneath her, she felt Manu pull in a deep breath.

She tightened her hold on him. "We'll find you a new one. A better one—"

He gripped her chin. "Kate."

She didn't stop to listen. "Whatever it takes, I'll—"

"Hey, look at me."

She looked into velvet-brown eyes. He was so strong and steady.

"I don't give a fuck about my leg."

Her mouth dropped open. "What?"

He shrugged. "You're alive. I'm alive. That's all I care about." He kissed her, and it wasn't a sweet, quick kiss. He deepened it, mastering her mouth, tongue delving deep.

"I see you're both feeling better," a dry, masculine voice said.

Kate let out a squeak of surprise. God, General Holmes had just caught her and Manu making out in the infirmary.

When she looked up, she swallowed a groan. It wasn't just Holmes. Alongside him stood Niko, Tane, Hemi, and Marcus. *Great.* She dropped her head to Manu's chest.

"I'm feeling pretty fucking great," Manu said.

There were deep chuckles in response.

"We wanted a quick debrief, and to give you an update," Holmes said.

Kate forced her head up.

"We cleaned out the abandoned mine," Marcus said. "No more raptors or their damn landmines."

"Fuckers," Hemi said. "We had fun running the last of them down."

"They'd been here, right under our noses for some time." Holmes face was composed, but Kate knew him well enough to know he was clearly pissed.

"It won't happen again," Niko added darkly.

"Manu, you now have a collection of alien landmines to study," Tane added. "We left them with your team."

Manu nodded. "I'll get to them, as soon as I'm back on my feet...or foot." He winked.

Kate made a choked sound. How the hell could he joke about this?

His lips quirked. "Too soon?"

Hemi roared with laughter, while the other men smiled.

Niko cleared his throat. "We're storing the landmines in a cordoned-off area in the old part of the Enclave that's been sectioned off the main base."

Kate knew they couldn't risk storing them in the heart of the Enclave. With Manu studying the functioning mines, they could learn a lot. Find a way to stop the damn things affecting their laser weapons, and maybe even use the tech against the aliens.

Emerson stepped forward. "There's something else. Manu, there was alien organic matter on your prosthetic."

"The scales," Kate said.

Emerson nodded. "It had started to embed into your skin as well, that's the main reason for the extra amputation. We're still studying it, but it was the same material we removed from Kendra's injuries."

"What?" Kate frowned. "This stuff is *in* the landmines?"

"Like a dirty biological bomb," Tane said. "The damn mines aren't just for blowing stuff up."

"Like I said, I'm still analyzing," the doc said. "But the landmines appear to spread alien DNA that searches for a host to infect."

Holmes ran a hand through his hair. "It appears the Gizzida aren't slowing down on their quest to turn us all into raptors."

"I'll keep working until I know more," Emerson added.

"Gabe happy about that?" Tane's dark gaze dropped to her belly.

Emerson pulled a face. "I'm pregnant, Tane. I don't need to be wrapped in cotton wool and locked away. I can still do my job."

"But it could be risky," the squad leader said. "Remember Chrissy nearly blew herself up studying that alien tech she removed from the Hunter engine."

"We have protocols in place," Emerson said. "We *have* to find out what the hell the aliens have cooked up now." Pain rippled over her face. "Or none of us, including my babies, will have a safe place to live."

"Keep us posted, Emerson," Holmes said.

Kate straightened, wishing like hell she wasn't wearing this stupid skimpy gown. "We used a cineole grenade. It caused the raptors to bleed."

All the men straightened.

"Really?" Marcus rasped.

Manu nodded. "Blood running out their eyes, noses, and mouths."

Emerson's face sharpened. "I'll let Noah know." She grinned. "We could be on to something."

"And the octagon?" Manu asked.

Niko shook his head and let out a frustrated breath. "Nothing."

Kate looked at him and then Holmes. "Permission to leave the Enclave for a scavenging mission. Manu needs a new prosthetic."

"No," Manu said.

"Manu—"

"I don't want you out there."

"And we need you back up and running."

A muscle ticked in his jaw. "Do you care if I have no leg?"

She gasped. "What? I don't care if you have no legs *and* no arms, Manu Rahia—"

He yanked her down and she slammed against his chest. His kiss was hard and unforgiving. More masculine chuckles rippled around them. Oh, she was entertaining everybody today.

She shifted off Manu. "Foolish man."

"No need for scavenging," Tane said. "When we got Manu's original prosthetic, we nabbed a few extras. We figured it couldn't hurt to have some backups or extras around."

Kate felt a burst of relief.

"We left them with Noah," Hemi said with a smile. "They'll probably be rocket-powered by now."

"Well, tell Noah to get a replacement to me," Emerson said, turning to look at Manu. "We can get you back up and running in no time."

Manu's arms tightened around Kate. "Actually, I'm not in a rush. I'm quite comfy here."

There were more chuckles, and Kate rolled her eyes as her chest filled with warmth.

CHAPTER SIXTEEN

"Okay, extend."

Manu followed Emerson's order, testing out his new prosthetic.

This one was racier than his old one. Noah had added quite a few enhancements.

"Good." The doc nodded and smiled. "The scans look great, and the function is good. It's successfully been embedded into your nerves. You'll need some rehab to get used to it, but I think it'll function even better than your previous one." She patted his shoulder. "You're cleared."

Manu stood, eager to get out of the infirmary. He'd been stuck in here two days. Kate visited and sat with him, but he wanted his woman to himself.

"Thanks, Doc."

She dusted her hands together. "All in a day's work around here."

"When you say all clear, you mean *all* clear, right?" he asked.

She waggled her eyebrows. "Yes, *all* clear." Then her face turned white.

"Emerson?" Manu stepped closer.

She waved him off. "If you don't want to see my breakfast make a reappearance, I suggest you go. Darn morning sickness."

He backed up a step. "Right. Thanks again."

Manu walked out of the infirmary with measured steps. He was moving a little slower than normal because he still needed to get used to the new prosthetic. His balance felt slightly different. He knew he had to get into the gym and work on his rehab. He figured he'd touch base with Kendra and see if she wanted to join him. The security officer had also had a new prosthetic attached yesterday.

But right now, Manu had other plans.

He nodded to a few people on the way, and finally made it to the Command Center. He passed through the big glass doors and headed straight for Kate's office. As he passed through the security room, he lifted his hand when a few people called out hellos to him.

He spotted Miles and nodded at her office. "She in there?"

Miles grinned. "Yep. Been acting damn jumpy all morning. Keeps threatening to call the infirmary for an update." The man's gaze dropped to Manu's legs. "Looks like it went well."

"Yeah. Kate's on a break for a bit."

Miles' grin widened and he tossed Manu a salute. "Roger that."

Manu stopped in the doorway and looked at her. She was on a call.

"Check it again." She paused. "I don't care, Dwayne. Check it three times if you have to. I want a full report on my desk by tonight." Pause. "Yes, by tonight. You think I care about your dinner plans? Good." She ended the call and looked up.

When she spotted him, she stood. She took her time scanning Manu's body and smiled. "Hey."

He held his arms out to his sides. "I'm up and mobile."

"Emerson cleared you?" Kate skirted her desk.

He shut the door behind him. Then he locked it.

Kate paused. "Manu—"

He strode toward her, and as soon as he was in reach, he gripped her hips and pressed his mouth to hers. She leaned into him, kissing him back. There was so much emotion in her embrace, and he wondered how anyone could ever think she was cool and unemotional.

He slid his hands under her ass and lifted her up onto her desk.

"We'd better check everything is in working order," he told her.

She slid her hands under his T-shirt. "Your leg got hurt, Rahia, not your—"

He pushed her back on the desk and she let out a small moan. He returned the favor, sliding his hands under her shirt and molding her breasts.

Manu set to work, so hungry for her. He plumped her breasts, tugged on her nipples, then leaned down, drawing one into his mouth. She was writhing beneath him.

"You're so hot, babe."

"Only for you."

Desire was a rough, edgy need pounding inside him. He quickly unbuttoned her trousers and yanked them off, along with her panties. Then he had his hands between her legs. Of course, she was wet for him. He pumped two fingers inside her, and she made small, husky cries. He thumbed her clit.

"You're all mine," he ground out.

"Yes."

"I color your world."

Her hot gaze met his. "Yes."

"So damn gorgeous, Kate."

He pushed her legs apart, loving that she had no inhibitions with him. Quickly, he unbuckled his belt and shoved his trousers down. He took his cock in hand and a second later, he thrust inside her.

She moaned, arching on her desk.

Manu had no finesse, no patience to make this last very long. He picked up his pace. This was a claiming. This was satisfying a savage need born in the desperate moments deep underground, when they'd fought together to survive.

"Give me your eyes, Kate."

She opened her eyes and their gazes met.

"There's nothing better than being inside you," he said.

"Faster." She reared up to grip his arms.

He grabbed her hands and pushed them above her

head on the desk. His hips kept hammering, his cock driving inside her. "Get there, babe."

He heard the change in her breathing, felt her sweet body tighten on his cock. She cried out, and he leaned down and pressed his mouth on hers, swallowing her cry.

Two more thrusts, and pleasure rushed through him. "Kate." A guttural cry as he poured himself inside her.

"Love you, Manu."

When he could function again, he was lying sprawled on top of her on the desk, panting.

Kate kissed the side of his neck. "I think your leg works just fine."

He laughed. Then he lifted his head and looked down at her flushed face.

"Marry me." The words came out of him unexpectedly.

"What?" She froze, looking like a deer in headlights.

"Marry me." It felt so right, those words echoing through him. "You're mine, I love you, and I'm too old for games. I want everyone to know that you're mine and I'm yours."

Her gaze moved over his face and then her expression softened. "You don't mess around, do you, Rahia?"

"Hell, no." He pulled her close. "I know when I'm onto a good thing."

"Me, too." She smiled. "Yes, I'll marry you, Manu."

"STILL NO SIGN OF THE OCTAGON," Elle said. "It's driving Marcus crazy."

Kate smoothed her hands down her dress, watching Elle and several other ladies sitting on chairs inside the small marquee set up in the Garden.

The women were all dressed up and sipping champagne. Outside, Kate could hear the murmur of voices and smelled the rich scent of grass and flowers.

From beside Elle, Liberty nodded, her coiffed blonde hair bobbing. "Adam, as well."

"We'll find it." This came from Mac. The tiny Squad Nine soldier was dolled up in a short blue dress. "The Gizzida can't hide it forever."

"I don't care what the aliens are doing." Kate pressed a hand to her churning belly. "I think I'm going to be sick."

"Not on the dress." Cam stepped up beside her, smoothing Kate's dress down. It was a simple column of ivory silk. When Kate had first looked in the mirror, she could hardly believe she looked so beautiful.

"Elle," Liberty said. "Adam said you found new references in raptor data to the Gizzida queen."

Everyone went quiet.

Elle nodded. "Nothing much. It doesn't say anything detailed about her, but she exists."

Cam stepped forward. "Well, I say fuck the Gizzida today. We have a wedding to enjoy."

Instantly, Kate's nerves surged. "I'm forty. I'm the head of security of a base filled with the survivors of an alien attack. I have no business getting married."

She heard giggles and looked at the gaggle of women watching her. They were sipping champagne—someone had raided the Enclave's supplies—and eating the canapés, all dressed in pretty dresses, like they didn't have a care in the world. Most of them were soldiers, for God's sake. They knew what was out there.

Cam gripped Kate's shoulder. "Are you in love with Manu Rahia?"

Kate's insides warmed. "Yes."

"Is he your badass?"

He sure was a badass and he was hers. "Yes."

"Are you his woman?"

Kate raised a brow. "I'm not sure I love that term, but yes."

"So, go out there and grab your happiness." Cam waved at the women. "We all know the sucky side of life, but when the good is right there in front of you, you hold on to it, and enjoy it every second you can. It carries you through the shitty times."

Kate nodded, feeling choked up.

Suddenly, Miles appeared in the marquee doorway. "Wow, you look gorgeous."

The man was dressed in a sharp suit, his sandy hair styled.

"Thanks," Kate said.

"When Manu sees you, he'll swallow his tongue."

Well, she had plans for his tongue, so she hoped not.

"It's time," Miles said.

From outside, Kate heard music start. The sweet sound of strings.

Oh, God. Her knees felt weak. She'd faced raptors in battle, but this reduced her to jelly.

Another figure ducked inside. Tane was wearing dark trousers, a crisp, white shirt, and no tie. His dreadlocks were pulled back and tied at the base of his neck. It was the most relaxed Kate had ever seen the Squad Three leader. Damn, he was incredibly handsome.

The women behind her let out some sighs.

"Don't you scrub up nicely," Cam called out.

Tane shot her a small smile. "I'm the good-looking brother."

Cam snorted. "Hemi might argue with you."

Tane looked at Kate. "Ready?"

Everything inside her steadied. She was committing herself to the man she loved. The bravest, strongest, most honorable man she'd ever met. "I'm ready."

Tane held out an arm, and she slipped hers through it. The women filed past her, giving her quick kisses.

The music swelled, and Kate let Tane lead her outside to the Garden, to walk her down the aisle. White chairs had been set out under the trees, with a red carpet running between them. Overhead, the retractable doors were open, letting sunshine spill down into the garden.

She saw the sea of faces—all the members of Hell Squad and their partners. Squad Nine. She saw Selena wearing a jewel-colored dress the same color as her eyes. Noah sat with his arm around his red-headed partner, Laura. Finn was grinning, holding Lia's hand. The berserkers were at the front, all of them looking handsome and dangerous.

"Thank you," Tane said quietly.

She looked up at him. "For what?"

"For making my brother happy. And helping him find the piece of himself that the aliens had stolen."

"It wasn't missing, just dented." She smiled. "He's the strongest man I know."

"Me, too." Tane led her toward the red carpet.

All Kate's focus went to the man waiting for her at the front with Holmes.

Manu stood straight and tall in a dark suit, white shirt bright against his bronze skin. Her gorgeous, hot guy. All hers.

His brown gaze stayed locked on her, and as the music swelled, Tane led her toward Manu. When they got close, Manu took two steps toward her, and pulled her toward him.

"Thanks, bro." He leaned down and nipped her lips.

The crowd laughed.

Holmes smiled. "Everyone ready for a wedding?"

The laughter turned to cheers and hollers. Kate smiled. Cam was right. This was why they fought, and this was what they had to hold on to, in order to keep up the fight.

Before all their friends and fellow survivors, Manu and Kate shared their vows. Her voice was strong and steady as she promised to be there for him, no matter what. To love him every day of their lives.

"I give you Mr. and Mrs. Rahia," Holmes announced.

Oh, God. Shock and excitement coursed through Kate.

Manu pulled her in and dramatically dipped her back over his arm, planting a deep kiss on her. Their friends cheered.

"Love you, babe," he murmured.

"I know," she said. "I love you right back."

With Manu, she was excited for every day. It didn't matter what the aliens did, what they had planned, what the hell the octagon device was. Kate had Manu, and that made everything better, brighter, and more colorful. It made life worth living.

"Who's ready to party?" Hemi called out.

Manu led Kate toward the tables loaded with food and drinks. Several people stopped to congratulate them. Each berserker lifted Kate off her feet and planted kisses on her. Most of them on the mouth.

As they walked under the trees, Kate spotted Kendra sitting on a chair, dressed in a flirty, pink dress. The woman was still getting used to her prosthetic leg, but she gave them a blinding smile and a wave.

"Save a dance for me, Captain," Kendra called out.

She smiled. "Sure thing, Kendra."

Manu pulled her to a stop. He looked over her head and nodded to someone.

She frowned. "What are you—?"

A second later, lights blinked on in the trees. A huge collection of colored lanterns, in all different shades. Kate gasped, and the guests all oohed and aahed.

Manu wrapped his arms around Kate. "I'll always bring color to your life, Kate. Just the same way you do for me."

Her chest filled with warmth, she leaned into her husband. "I love you, Manu." And under the colored lights, Manu kissed his wife.

I hope you enjoyed Manu and Kate's story!

Hell Squad continues with GRIFF, starring former cop and ex-con Griff and feisty comms officer Indy. Coming in 2019.

But Anna, 2019 is really far away! I know, I know. But I have two new action-packed romance series on the way to help with the wait. And I promise Hell Squad will be back with a bang before you know it.

For more action-packed romance, read on for a preview of the first chapter of *Gladiator,* the first book in my best-winning Galactic Gladiators series.

Don't miss out! For updates about new releases, action romance info, free books, and other fun stuff, sign up for my VIP mailing list and get your *free box set* containing three action-packed romances.

Visit here to get started: www.annahackettbooks.com

FREE BOX SET DOWNLOAD

JOIN THE ACTION-PACKED ADVENTURE!

PREVIEW: GLADIATOR

MORE SCI-FI ROMANCE

Fighting for love, honor, and freedom on the galaxy's lawless outer rim.

Fighting for love, honor, and freedom on the galaxy's lawless outer rim...

When Earth space marine Harper Adams finds herself abducted by alien slavers off a space station, her life turns into a battle for survival. Dumped into an arena on a desert planet on the outer rim, she finds herself face to face with a big, tattooed alien gladiator...the champion of the Kor Magna Arena.

A former prince abandoned to the arena as a teen, Raiden Tiago has long ago earned his freedom. Now he rules the arena, but he doesn't fight for the glory, but instead for his own dark purpose—revenge against the Thraxian aliens who destroyed his planet. Then his existence is rocked by one small, fierce female fighter from an unknown planet called Earth.

Harper is determined to find a way home, but when she spots her best friend in the arena—a slave of the evil Thraxian aliens—she'll do anything to save her friend... even join forces with the tough, alpha male who sets her body on fire. But as Harper and Raiden step foot onto the blood-soaked sands of the arena, Harper worries that Raiden has his own dangerous agenda...

Just another day at the office.

Harper Adams pulled herself along the outside of the space station module. She could hear her quiet breathing inside her spacesuit, and she easily pulled her weightless body along the slick, white surface of the module. She stopped to check a security panel, ensuring all the systems were running smoothly.

Check. Same as it had been yesterday, and the day before that. But Harper never ever let herself forget that they were six hundred million kilometers away from Earth. That meant they were dependent only on themselves. She tapped some buttons on the security panel before closing the reinforced plastic cover. She liked to dot all her *I*s and cross all her *T*s. She never left anything to chance.

She grabbed the handholds and started pulling

herself up over the cylindrical pod to check the panels on the other side. Glancing back behind herself, she caught a beautiful view of the planet below.

Harper stopped and made herself take it all in. The orange, white, and cream bands of Jupiter could take your breath away. Today, she could even see the famous super-storm of the Great Red Spot. She'd been on the Fortuna Research Station for almost eighteen months. That meant, despite the amazing view, she really didn't see it anymore.

She turned her head and looked down the length of the space station. At the end was the giant circular donut that housed the main living quarters and offices. The main ring rotated to provide artificial gravity for the residents. Lying off the center of the ring was the long cylinder of the research facility, and off that cylinder were several modules that housed various scientific labs and storage. At the far end of the station was the docking area for the supply ships that came from Earth every few months.

"Lieutenant Adams? Have you finished those checks?"

Harper heard the calm voice of her fellow space marine and boss, Captain Samantha Santos, through the comm system in her helmet.

"Almost done," Harper answered.

"Take a good look at the botany module. The computer's showing some strange energy spikes, but the scientists in there said everything looks fine. Must be a system malfunction."

Which meant the geek squad engineers were going to have to come in and do some maintenance. "On it."

Harper swung her body around, and went feet-first down the other side of the module. She knew the rest of the security team—all made up of United Nations Space Marines—would be running similar checks on the other modules across the station. They had a great team to ensure the safety of the hundreds of scientists aboard the station. There was also a dedicated team of engineers that kept the guts of the station running.

She passed a large, solid window into the module, and could see various scientists floating around benches filled with all kinds of plants. They all wore matching gray jumpsuits accented with bright-blue at the collars, that indicated science team. There was a vast mix of scientists and disciplines aboard—biologists, botanists, chemists, astronomers, physicists, medical experts, and the list went on. All of them were conducting experiments, and some were searching for alien life beyond the edge of the solar system. It seemed like every other week, more probes were being sent out to hunt for radio signals or collect samples.

Since humans had perfected large solar sails as a way to safely and quickly propel spacecraft, getting around the solar system had become a lot easier. With radiation pressure exerted by sunlight onto the mirrored sails, they could travel from Earth to Fortuna Station orbiting Jupiter in just a few months. And many of the scientists aboard the station were looking beyond the solar system, planning manned expeditions farther and farther away. Harper wasn't sure they were quite ready for that.

She quickly checked the adjacent control panel. Among all the green lights, she spotted one that was blinking red, and she frowned. They definitely had a problem with the locking system on the exterior door at the end of the module. She activated the small propulsion pack on her spacesuit, and circled around the module. She slowed down as she passed the large, round exterior door at the end of the cylindrical module.

It was all locked into place and looked secure.

As she moved back to the module, she grabbed a handhold and then tapped the small tablet attached to the forearm of her suit. She keyed in a request for maintenance to come and check it.

She looked up and realized she was right near another window. Through the reinforced glass, a pretty, curvy blonde woman looked up and spotted Harper. She smiled and waved. Harper couldn't help but smile and lifted her gloved hand in greeting.

Dr. Regan Forrest was a botanist and a few years younger than Harper. The young woman was so open and friendly, and had befriended Harper from her first day on the station. Harper had never had a lot of friends —mainly because she'd been too busy raising her younger sister and working. She'd never had time for girly nights out or gossip.

But Regan was friendly, smart, and had the heart of a steamroller under her pretty exterior. Harper always had trouble saying no to her. Maybe the woman reminded her a little of Brianna. At the thought of her sister, something twisted painfully in Harper's chest.

Regan floated over to the window and held up a small tablet. She'd typed in some words.

Cards tonight?

Harper had been teaching Regan how to play poker. The woman was terrible at it, and Harper beat her all the time. But Regan never gave up.

Harper nodded and held up two fingers to indicate a couple of hours. She was off-shift shortly, and then she had a sparring match with Regan's cousin, Rory—one of the station engineers—in the gym. Aurora "Call me Rory or I'll hit you" Fraser had been trained in mixed martial arts, and Harper found the female engineer a hell of a sparring partner. Rory was teaching Harper some martial arts moves and Harper was showing the woman some basic sword moves. Since she was little, Harper had been a keen fencer.

Regan grinned back and nodded. Then the woman's wide smile disappeared. She spun around, and through the glass Harper could see the other scientists all looking around, concerned. One scientist was spinning around, green plants floating in the air around him, along with fat droplets of water and some other green fluid. He'd clearly screwed up and let his experiment get free.

"Lieutenant Adams?" The captain's voice came through her helmet again. "Harper?"

There was a sense of urgency that made Harper's belly tighten. "Go ahead, Captain."

"We have an alarm sounding in the botany module. The computer says there is a risk of decompression."

Dammit. "I just checked the security panels. The

locking mechanism on the exterior door is showing red. I did a visual inspection and it's closed up tight."

"Okay, we talked with the scientist in charge. Looks like one of her team let something loose in there. It isn't dangerous, but it must be messing with the alarm sensors. System's locked them all in there." She made an annoyed sound. "Idiots will have to stay there until engineering can get down there and free them."

Harper studied the room through the glass again. Some of the green liquid had floated over to another bench that contained various frothing cylinders on it. A second later, the cylinders shattered, their contents bubbling upward.

The scientists all moved to the back exit of the module, banging on the locked door. *Damn.* They were trapped.

Harper met Regan's gaze. Her friend's face was pale, and wisps of her blonde hair had escaped her ponytail, floating around her face.

"Captain," Harper said. "Something's wrong. The experiments have overflowed their containment." She could see the scientists were all coughing.

"Engineering is on the way," the captain said.

Harper pushed herself off, flying over the surface of the module. She reached the control panel and saw that several other lights had turned red. They needed to get this under control and they needed to do it now.

"Harper!" The captain's panicked voice. "Decompression in progress!"

What the hell? The module jerked beneath Harper.

She looked up and saw the exterior door blow off, flying away from the station.

Her heart stopped. That meant all the scientists were exposed to the vacuum of space.

Fuck. Harper pushed off again, sending herself flying toward the end of the module. She put her arms by her sides to help increase her speed. Through the window, she saw that most of the scientists had grabbed on to whatever they could hold on to. A few were pulling emergency breathers over their heads.

She reached the end of the pod and saw the damage. There was torn metal where the door had been ripped off. Inside the door, she knew there would be a temporary repair kit containing a sheet of high-tech nano fabric that could be stretched across the opening to reestablish pressure. But it needed to be put in place manually. Harper reached for the latch to release the repair kit.

Suddenly, a slim body shot out of the pod, her arms and legs kicking. Her mouth was wide open in a silent scream.

Regan. Harper didn't let herself think. She turned, pushed off and fired her propulsion system, arrowing after her friend.

"Security Team to the botany module," she yelled through her comm system. "Security Team to botany module. We have decompression. One scientist has been expelled. I'm going after her. I need someone that can help calm the others and get the module sealed again."

"Acknowledged, Lieutenant," Captain Santos answered. "I'm on my way."

Harper focused on reaching Regan. She was gaining on her. She saw that the woman had lost consciousness. She also knew that Regan had only a couple of minutes to survive out here. Harper let her training take over. She tapped the propulsion system controls, trying for more speed, as she maneuvered her way toward Regan.

As she got close, Harper reached out and wrapped her arm around the scientist. "I've got you."

Harper turned, at the same time clipping a safety line to the loops on Regan's jumpsuit. Then, she touched the controls and propelled them straight back towards the module. She kept her friend pulled tightly toward her chest. *Hold on, Regan.*

She was so still. It reminded Harper of holding Brianna's dead body in her arms. Harper's jaw tightened. She wouldn't let Regan die out here. The woman had dreamed of working in space, and worked her entire career to get here, even defying her family. Harper wasn't going to fail her.

As the module got closer, she saw that the security team had arrived. She saw the captain's long, muscled body as she and another man put up the nano fabric.

"Incoming. Keep the door open."

"Can't keep it open much longer, Adams," the captain replied. "Make it snappy."

Harper adjusted her course, and, a second later, she shot through the door with Regan in her arms. Behind her, the captain and another huge security marine, Lieutenant Blaine Strong, pulled the stretchy fabric across the opening.

"Decompression contained," the computer intoned.

Harper released a breath. On the panel beside the door, she saw the lights turning green. The nano fabric wouldn't hold forever, but it would do until they got everyone out of here, and then got a maintenance team in here to fix the door.

"Oxygen levels at required levels," the computer said again.

"Good work, Lieutenant." Captain Sam Santos floated over. She was a tall woman with a strong face and brown hair she kept pulled back in a tight ponytail. She had curves she kept ruthlessly toned, and golden skin she always said was thanks to her Puerto Rican heritage.

"Thanks, Captain." Harper ripped her helmet off and looked down at Regan.

Her blonde hair was a wild tangle, her face was pale and marked by what everyone who worked in space called space hickeys—bruises caused by the skin's small blood vessels bursting when exposed to the vacuum of space. *Please be okay.*

"Here." Blaine appeared, holding a portable breather. The big man was an excellent marine. He was about six foot five with broad shoulders that stretched his spacesuit to the limit. She knew he was a few inches over the height limit for space operations, but he was a damn good marine, which must have gone in his favor. He had dark skin thanks to his African-American father and his handsome face made him popular with the station's single ladies, but mostly he worked and hung out with the other marines.

"Thanks." Harper slipped the clear mask over Regan's mouth.

"Nice work out there." Blaine patted her shoulder. "She's alive because of you."

Suddenly, Regan jerked, pulling in a hard breath.

"You're okay." Harper gripped Regan's shoulder. "Take it easy."

Regan looked around the module, dazed and panicky. Harper watched as Regan caught sight of the fabric stretched across the end of the module, and all the plants floating around inside.

"God," Regan said with a raspy gasp, her breath fogging up the dome of the breather. She shook her head, her gaze moving to Harper. "Thanks, Harper."

"Any time." Harper squeezed her friend's shoulder. "It's what I'm here for."

Regan managed a wan smile. "No, it's just you. You didn't have to fly out into space to rescue me. I'm grateful."

"Come on. We need to get you to the infirmary so they can check you out. Maybe put some cream on your hickeys."

"Hickeys?" Regan touched her face and groaned. "Oh, no. I'm going to get a ribbing."

"And you didn't even get them the pleasurable way."

A faint blush touched Regan's cheeks. "That's right. If I had, at least the ribbing would have been worth it."

With a relieved laugh, Harper looked over at her captain. "I'm going to get Regan to the infirmary."

The other woman nodded. "Good. We'll meet you back at the Security Center."

With a nod, Harper pushed off, keeping one arm around Regan, and they floated into the main part of the science facility. Soon, they moved through the entrance into the central hub of the space station. As the artificial gravity hit, Harper's boots thudded onto the floor. Beside her, Regan almost collapsed.

Harper took most of the woman's weight and helped her down the corridor. They pushed into the infirmary.

A gray-haired, barrel-chested man rushed over. "Decided to take an unscheduled spacewalk, Dr. Forrest?"

Regan smiled weakly. "Yes. Without a spacesuit."

The doctor made a tsking sound and then took her from Harper. "We'll get her all patched up."

Harper nodded. "I'll come and check on you later."

Regan grabbed her hand. "We have a blackjack game scheduled. I'm planning to win back all those chocolates you won off me."

Harper snorted. "You can try." It was good to see some life back in Regan's blue eyes.

As Harper strode out into the corridor, she ran a hand through her dark hair, tension slowly melting out of her shoulders. She really needed a beer. She tilted her neck one way and then the other, hearing the bones pop.

Just another day at the office. The image of Regan drifting away from the space station burst in her head. Harper released a breath. She was okay. Regan was safe and alive. That was all that mattered.

With a shake of her head, Harper headed toward the Security Center. She needed to debrief with the captain and clock off. Then she could get out of her spacesuit and take the one-minute shower that they were all allotted.

That was the one thing she missed about Earth. Long, hot showers.

And swimming. She'd been a swimmer all her life and there were days she missed slicing through the water.

She walked along a long corridor, meeting a few people—mainly scientists. She reached a spot where there was a long bank of windows that afforded a lovely view of Jupiter, and space beyond it.

Stingy showers and unscheduled spacewalks aside, Harper had zero regrets about coming out into space. There'd been nothing left for her on Earth, and to her surprise, she'd made friends here on Fortuna.

As she stared out into the black, mesmerized by the twinkle of stars, she caught a small flash of light in the distance. She paused, frowning. What the hell was that?

She stared hard at the spot where she'd seen the flash. Nothing there but the pretty sprinkle of stars. Harper shook her head. Fatigue was playing tricks on her. It had to have just been a weird trick of the lights reflecting off the glass.

Pushing the strange sighting away, she continued on to the Security Center.

Galactic Gladiators

Gladiator

Warrior

Hero

Protector

Champion

Barbarian
Beast
Rogue
Guardian
Cyborg
Also Available as Audiobooks!

PREVIEW: AMONG GALACTIC RUINS

MORE ACTION ROMANCE?

**ACTION
ADVENTURE
TREASURE HUNTS
SEXY SCI-FI ROMANCE**

When astro-archeologist and museum curator Dr. Lexa Carter discovers a secret map to a lost old Earth treasure—a priceless Fabergé egg—she's excited at the prospect of a treasure hunt to the dangerous desert planet of Zerzura. What she's not so happy about is being saddled with a bodyguard—the museum's mysterious new head of security, Damon Malik.

After many dangerous years as a galactic spy, Damon

Malik just wanted a quiet job where no one tried to kill him. Instead of easy work in a museum full of artifacts, he finds himself on a backwater planet babysitting the most infuriating woman he's ever met.

She thinks he's arrogant. He thinks she's a trouble-magnet. But among the desert sands and ruins, adventure led by a young, brash treasure hunter named Dathan Phoenix, takes a deadly turn. As it becomes clear that someone doesn't want them to find the treasure, Lexa and Damon will have to trust each other just to survive.

The Phoenix Adventures

Among Galactic Ruins
At Star's End
In the Devil's Nebula
On a Rogue Planet
Beneath a Trojan Moon
Beyond Galaxy's Edge
On a Cyborg Planet
Return to Dark Earth
On a Barbarian World
Lost in Barbarian Space
Through Uncharted Space
Crashed on an Ice World

ALSO BY ANNA HACKETT

Treasure Hunter Security

Undiscovered

Uncharted

Unexplored

Unfathomed

Untraveled

Unmapped

Galactic Gladiators

Gladiator

Warrior

Hero

Protector

Champion

Barbarian

Beast

Rogue

Guardian

Cyborg

Also Available as Audiobooks!

Hell Squad

Marcus

Cruz

Gabe

Reed

Roth

Noah

Shaw

Holmes

Niko

Finn

Theron

Hemi

Ash

Levi

Also Available as Audiobooks!

The Anomaly Series

Time Thief

Mind Raider

Soul Stealer

Salvation

Anomaly Series Box Set

The Phoenix Adventures

Among Galactic Ruins

At Star's End

In the Devil's Nebula

On a Rogue Planet

Beneath a Trojan Moon

Beyond Galaxy's Edge

On a Cyborg Planet

Return to Dark Earth

On a Barbarian World

Lost in Barbarian Space

Through Uncharted Space

Crashed on an Ice World

Perma Series

Winter Fusion

A Galactic Holiday

Warriors of the Wind

Tempest

Storm & Seduction

Fury & Darkness

Standalone Titles

Savage Dragon

Hunter's Surrender

One Night with the Wolf

For more information visit AnnaHackettBooks.com

ABOUT THE AUTHOR

I'm a USA Today bestselling author and I'm passionate about **_action romance_**. I love stories that combine the thrill of falling in love with the excitement of action, danger and adventure. I'm a sucker for that moment when the team is walking in slow motion, shoulder-to-shoulder heading off into battle. I write about people overcoming unbeatable odds and achieving seemingly impossible goals. I like to believe it's possible for all of us to do the same.

My books are mixture of action, adventure and sexy romance and they're recommended for anyone who enjoys fast-paced stories where the boy wins the girl at the end (or sometimes the girl wins the boy!)

For release dates, action romance info, free books, and other fun stuff, sign up for the latest news here:

Website: www.annahackettbooks.com